Zip, Zero, Zilch

by Tammy Falkner

Night Shift Publishing

For Amy

Copyright © 2014 by Tammy Falkner

Zip, Zero, Zilch
Print Edition
Night Shift Publishing
Cover design by Tammy Falkner
Cover photo by © Monkey Business Images | Dreamstime.com
ISBN-13: 978-1503319486
ISBN-10: 1503319482

This book is a work of fiction. Names, characters, places, and incidents either are products of the author's imagination or are used fictitiously. Any resemblance to actual persons, living or dead, events, or locales is entirely coincidental.

Peck

My phone buzzes and I ignore it. It's just one of my sisters. The guy in the sound booth shoots me a dirty look. I'm working on a track for the new album, because I want to see how some new beats sound mixed with our new single. He hits a button. "Do you need to take a break?" he asks.

I shake my head and keep playing. I play drums for a band, and I don't have time to stop right now. Anything my sisters have to say can wait until I'm done here.

My phone rumbles again.

"Let's call it quits, shall we?" he says from the booth.

Sometimes it's hell having four sisters. And sometimes it's awesome. Right now I'm annoyed. I pick up my phone but instead of answering it I cram it into my pocket.

I go out into the sound area and sit down next to the recording engineer. "Let me hear it one time, will you?" I tap my drumsticks lightly on the table while I talk.

He mixes it all up, and music comes into the headset he gives me. I like it. I like it a lot. I smile at him and nod.

He smiles back. "It's better," he says. "You were right." He shakes his head.

"Don't look so happy about it," I tease. I take the headphones off and lay them on the counter. I swipe a hand down my face.

My phone rings again, just as the door opens. It flies inward, slamming hard against the wall. I jump to my feet when my sister Lark comes sliding into the room.

"Oh, my God, I have been trying to call you for an *hour*," she blurts out. She bends at the waist, trying to catch her breath. She stands up, pressing a hand to her side.

"What's wrong?" I ask.

"I can't breathe," she pants. She holds up one finger. "Stairs." She gulps air.

One of her gloves slips down her wrist, and that's when I realize how serious this is. Lark never takes her gloves off. She never lets anyone see her hands or arms. Ever. For a long time, I thought she was just a germ freak—until I learned the truth. But the fact that she just let her glove slip tells me a lot. "Did someone die?" I ask.

She nods. But then she shakes her head. Then she nods again.

"Oh, my God!" I cover my mouth with my hand. "Who?"

"Sam Reed," she pants out.

My heart lurches. My stomach dips and blackness crowds the corners of my vision.

"Emily just called to say he was in a really bad accident. They're all on their way back from the beach to go to the hospital."

I sink into a chair. "And he *died?*" How could he? We have unfinished business.

She waves a hand through the air. "No, no, not yet."

I jump up. "Then why the hell did you tell me he was dead?"

"At the time, I was trying to breathe!" she yells back. "It's not my fault you misunderstood!"

The door flies open again and another of my sisters runs into the room. Finally. Someone who can make sense of it.

"Emily just called again," Wren says. "They just got to the hospital and Sam is in surgery." Wren might be a mess on the outside, but she's got it together on the inside. Thank God.

I jab my drumsticks into my back pocket and start for the door.

"Where are you going?" Wren calls to my back.

I don't wait for her. I hail a cab and get in it, my heart beating about a mile a minute. Sam's in the hospital. In surgery. I left things at a bad place the last time I saw him. A really bad place. I can't stand the idea of him being injured and possibly dying without knowing how I truly feel about him.

***

The cab stops at the Emergency Room doors, and I get out. I go to the desk, and they tell me where the waiting room is for surgery, and I go in that direction. "Are you one of them?" the lady at reception asks me.

I lift my brow at her, because I can't get my thoughts together enough to talk.

"There are a lot of them here for him." I look blankly at her. "His family."

Oh, yeah. There are a lot of Reeds, and all of them in one place can be a little intimidating. Lots of big, blond, tatted-up men. Like a buffet of testosterone and hotness, wrapped in pretty ink.

I stop in the doorway of the waiting area. I can hear the low murmur of male voices and stick my head into the room. The Reed brothers are all over the place, not to mention their wives. I find Emily and motion toward her. She waves me into the room.

I sit down beside her and she takes my hand. *How bad is it?* I ask her in sign language. Emily's husband, Logan, is deaf, so the whole family signs. Thank God these people speak my language. Because if I opened my mouth right now, one big long stutter would come out, and nothing else.

Pretty bad, she replies.

What happened?

She shrugs and shakes her head. *He left the beach right after the wedding to go home. He had to get to practice. He'd already missed way too much training time. And on the way from the airport to his house, he was in an accident.*

Can I do anything?

"Pray," Paul says from behind her.

Well, there's that. I nod. *Anything else?*

She shakes her head.

Pete is sitting across the room with his elbows on his knees, his face buried in his hands. Reagan rubs his back and talks softly into his ear. He nods, albeit reluctantly, and kisses her quickly, pulling her against him for a hug. She falls into his arms, like she's meant to be there.

Is it okay if I stay for a little while? I ask.

Emily squeezes my hand. "Of course."

There's a commotion in the hallway and my four sisters come into the room. They're on their tiptoes almost, trying to be quiet. Emily gives them the story, and they sit down beside one another on the floor and lean against the wall.

The Reeds take people in like they're family. Anyone. The only requirement is that you have a pulse. And if you don't have a heart, they'll give you theirs. So my sisters and I already feel a connection here, but I can't help but think that we should leave and give them some privacy.

"Where are the kids?" Lark asks.

"With a sitter," Friday says.

"All of them?"

There are a lot of Reed kids too. Paul and Friday have two—three if you count Jacob. And Matt and Sky have four little ones plus Seth. Emily and Logan have one.

Matt sniggers. "You say it like we have our own circus."

"Well, if the shoe fits," Lark says.

Pete holds up a finger. "That would be shoes—plural. Lots of circus animals."

Do you want us to go and take care of the kids? I ask. *We'd be happy to.*

Sky, Matt's wife, shakes her head. "We're going to go home as soon as we find out what's happening. He's going to be fine. I'm certain." She squeezes my hand.

Ten bucks says the wives might go home, but the brothers won't. Or at least not all of them.

A man in green scrubs walks into the room. "Reed family?" he asks.

"Here," they all say at once. The doctor looks around the room and shakes his head.

"Immediate family?" he asks.

"Here," they all say at once again.

"Get on with it," Paul barks.

"Your brother is a very lucky man," the doctor says as he pulls his glasses from his face and brushes a finger over the bridge of his nose. "He broke his tibia—one of the bones in the lower leg—in the crash, and has a pretty bad head laceration. We stitched him up, set the leg, put him in a cast, and we're going to need to keep him at least overnight."

"Why?" Pete asks.

"The team physician wants us to keep an eye on him."

So they know who he is. And what he does.

"How did the *team* know?"

The doctor shrugs. "I called them." He glares at us. "He plays pro ball." He says it like it's the Holy Grail. "They're sending the team physician to evaluate him in the morning."

The door bursts open, and a couple of men and a few women walk into the room. They're loud and noisy and they're extremely disrespectful.

"Will he still be able to play?" one of them asks.

The doctor shakes his head. "He's going to be on the bench for a while. It's a damn shame, too."

Paul swipes a hand down his face and takes a deep breath.

"Some players come back from an injury like this," the doctor says helpfully.

Oh, hell, there's a chance he might not play again?

"Can we see him?" Pete asks.

"One at a time," the doctor says with a nod.

"Which way?" Pete barks. The doctor points.

Pete takes Reagan's hand and drags her down the hallway.

"Only one!" the doctor calls.

"We are only one," Pete yells back, but he doesn't stop.

"Matt, you should go next," Paul says. "You have kids to get back home to."

Matt nods, but he says, "So do you."

"I'm going to hang out for a while anyway."

"You know Pete's not going to go home tonight," Matt says.

Paul nods. "I know."

Pete and Sam are twins. They have a bond.

The doctor shakes hands with Paul and leaves the room. The people who came in last swarm Paul, asking questions. It turns out they're from the team. And the girls are cheerleaders.

"Only family can visit," Paul warns.

"We know," one of the girls says. "We heard about the accident and just wanted to come and check on him. We won't stay long."

I sit down beside my sisters. "Y-you should go h-home," I say to them quietly. I talk to my sisters. I always have. My stutter isn't as bad when I talk to them. Not as bad as it is with anyone else.

"We'll wait," Lark says. She leans the back of her head against the wall, and tilts it so that she can look at me. She takes my hand and gives it a squeeze. "He's going to be fine," she says.

I take a breath.

I sit quietly as his brothers come and go. Pete and Reagan come out, and Matt and Sky go in. And the cycle continues until everyone has had a visit. Pete kisses Reagan goodbye. It looks like he's going to spend the night after all. "This is a pretty sucky wedding night," he tells her.

"You'll make up for it later," she teases him. He hugs her, and then walks her and the rest of them out to waiting cabs.

When Pete comes back, I stand up and wipe off the butt of my pants. I should go home. I can do nothing for anyone here.

Pete motions toward the hallway. "Come on," he says. He doesn't want the team members or the cheerleaders to see me. I sneak to the doorway and follow him down the hall. The smell of disinfectant tickles my nose.

When we get to Sam's room, he's sitting up, but his eyes are closed.

I don't want to wake him, I sign.

He smiles. "You're the only one he asked for."

My heart thuds. *He asked for me?*

He nods. "He's a little fucked up." He grins. "Okay, a *lot* fucked up."

I walk into the room and sit down in the chair beside the bed. Sam's hand lies outside the covers, so I take it in mine. I can see the veins in his hand, stark against his too-pale skin, and I move his IV line over so I don't bump it.

Sam's hand suddenly squeezes mine. I look up and find him smiling at me. It's a goofy grin, and I'm so damn happy to see it that tears fill my eyes.

"Don't cry, cupcake," he says softly.

His eyes are barely open, and they shaved part of his head.

"I'm so glad you're okay," I whisper. I tap my thumb on the bedrail, so I can talk without stuttering.

"It'll take more than a semi truck with a drunk driver to take me out, cupcake." He laughs, but then he clutches his head. "That hurt," he murmurs.

"Can I do anything for you?" *Tap. Tap.*

"Just stay for a little while."

I scoot my chair closer.

"Where's Pete?" he asks.

"I don't know." *Tap. Tap.*

"He got married today. And I fucked his honeymoon all up."

"He doesn't seem to mind." *Tap. Tap.*

He whispers fiercely, "He's s'posed to be getting laid!"

I laugh. I can't help it. "He'd rather be here."

"If I had a choice between having newly-wed, wall-banging, awesomely good sex and hanging out with me, I wouldn't pick me. I'd be at home fucking Reagan." His face turns a little green. "Well, *I* wouldn't fuck Reagan, because that would be gross. But Pete should be home fucking Reagan."

His words are slurred and I can tell they've given him pain meds. But he still makes me laugh.

"Hey cupcake!" he says, like he just had a great idea. "I'm so glad you're here."

"Me too," I say.

"I thought you were ready to kick me to the curb."

I was. But when I found out he was hurt, it nearly gutted me. "Would if I could," I say.

"Do you think you could fall in love with me, cupcake?" he blurts out.

I'm startled. I know he's medicated, so I shouldn't put any stock into his words, but I can't help it. "You should get some rest," I say. *Tap. Tap.*

"So, that would be a no." He whistles. Then he scrunches up his face when it makes his head hurt. "I'm in trouble," he whispers quietly.

"What?"

He squeezes my hand. "I'm pretty sure I'm in love with you, cupcake," he says. "I just wish you could love me back."

"You've had a lot of pain meds," I say.

Suddenly, he grabs the neck of my shirt and jerks me so that I fall over his chest. His lips are right next to mine. "Listen to me," he says.

"Okay," I whisper.

"I don't have much going for me, but I know what love feels like."

"How?"

"It just is, cupcake. You don't get to pick who you fall in love with. And God knows, if my head could pick, it wouldn't be you."

I push back to get off his chest, because I'm offended. But he holds me tight.

"You're not easy to love, because you can't love me back. But you might one day. I'll wait. But you got to start taking my calls." He cups the back of my head and brings my face toward his. A cough from the doorway startles us apart. I stand up and pull my shirt down where he rucked it up.

"Visiting hours are over," a nurse says.

"She's not a visitor," he says. She comes and inserts a needle into his IV, and his eyes close. He doesn't open them when he says, "She's going to marry me one day. She just doesn't know it yet." His head falls to the side and he starts to softly snore. His hand goes slack around mine.

I pull back, my heart skipping like mad.

"They say some of the most ridiculous things when they're medicated." The nurse shakes her head. "He probably won't remember any of this tomorrow."

Pete comes into the room. "Everything okay?" he asks. He looks from Sam to me and back.

"Just gave him some pain meds," the nurse says.

I'm going to go, I sign to him. I turn back when I get to the door. *Will you call if anything goes…wrong?*

He nods. "I'm going to go get some coffee while he's asleep."

I go to the public bathroom and sink back against the wall. He was medicated. He didn't mean any of that. Did he? He couldn't have. I stand there until my heart stops feeling like it's going to jump out of my chest. I need to go and tell him that I do have feelings for him. What if something goes wrong during the night and I can't tell him tomorrow? I need for him to know.

I go back to his room and stop in the doorway. Sitting beside his bed is a girl. She's holding his hand and talking to him. He smiles at her and says, "I'm serious. I'm going to marry you."

My heart jolts. He may as well have stabbed me with a knife.

I turn and leave. I don't run into Pete, and my sisters are waiting for me.

"What happened?" Lark asks when we get in the cab.

I wipe a tear from my cheek as it snakes a warm path down my face. "N-nothing."

"Did you talk to him?"

I nod.

"And?" Wren chirps.

"A-and the ch-cheerleader is in with him now."

"Oh," Wren says.

"Yeah," I say.

I'm an idiot.

Peck

When I was twelve, I went for months thinking I was dead. Everyone in my household ignored me. That was per my mother. "If she won't speak, don't speak to her," she'd said. What she didn't understand was that I wanted to speak. I wanted to speak with a desperation unlike any other. I wanted to unburden my mind. I *wanted* to talk.

I just couldn't.

So I moved around the house, prepared my own meals, got myself on the bus and off, took care of my own laundry, and I spent most of my time in my room, since no one was going to talk to me anyway.

I thought I was dead. Because why else would they not speak to me? Why would they punish me like they did for something I couldn't control? I must have died and someone forgot to tell me. I was a ghostly specter of myself.

My mother and her boyfriend spent more time away from home than in the small apartment my mom and I shared. He kept a place across town, and it became easier for her to stay there rather than come home. I didn't mind. I was a ghost walking around alone anyway, right? I spent my nights alone and was grateful for the silence. Because it would still be silent even if she were here.

But then there was a problem one day at school, and I ended up in the emergency room and then had my appendix out. It took them four days to find my mother, and suddenly someone cared if I lived or died.

Her name was Mrs. Derricks, and she was the school counselor. She brought me into her office and changed my life that day, and every day since.

The door slamming behind me jerks me from my thoughts of Mrs. Derricks.

Why aren't you dressed? I ask Lark in sign language as she drops her things on the couch and flops down.

"Dressed for what?" she asks, blowing out a breath.

For the funeral.

Her brow furrows. "What funeral?"

My hands fly wildly. *Mrs. Derricks' funeral!*

"Oh, crap," she says. She jumps up. "Totally forgot. Give me five minutes to change."

I text Wren and Star to see where they are, but just as I hit send, they come through the door. They couldn't be more opposite. They're sisters, born one year apart. And while they look alike, they couldn't be more different.

"You need to tie your shoe," Star says to Wren.

Wren looks down. "Why?"

"Because you'll trip over it."

"Who cares," Wren tosses back.

Star has her shirt tucked into a pair of nice pants, her creases all perfect and sharp. Wren, on the other hand, is wearing jeans and a T-shirt I think she stole from Emilio when we stayed over with him and Marta at their house for Christmas. It's four sizes too big for her and hangs down almost to her knees.

Emilio Vasquez isn't our real dad. He's the man who "sprung us from jail" as he calls it. In reality, it was a group home, but he's pretty accurate. He and his wife Marta couldn't have kids, so they decided to use their millions to better the life of a child. And they ended up with five of us, all at once.

Emilio is a former rock and roll star who hung up his microphone when drugs and drinking destroyed his band. Marta is a former groupie he fell in love with, or that's at least how he tells it. She smacks the back of his head every time he calls her a groupie. She's a tiny little Latina fireball.

To us, they're our parents. They're the family we weren't born with, but were lucky enough to grow into.

"I can't find black gloves!" Lark calls from her room.

"Why do you need black gloves?" Wren yells back.

"For the funeral!" Lark bellows.

"Oh, shit." Wren streaks to her room with Star right behind her. They forgot too, apparently.

Five minutes later, they all come out dressed in dark colors. Wren looks like a slouch, but a respectable slouch. Star looks like she could be walking a runway.

"Tie your shoe," Star says to Wren.

"Why?" Wren asks.

Do we really have to do this every day? When we lived with Emilio and Marta, their solid presences kept the fighting down. But now that we're on our own, my sisters snipe at one another like verbal fencing is their favorite pastime.

I tap my finger on the counter, because when I tap, I can speak without a stammer. "Has anyone seen Fin?" I ask.

Star shakes her head and squats down to tie Wren's shoe.

"Can't stand it, can you?" Wren taunts.

"Shut up," Star grumbles. She pulls a brush from the tidy little purse she has hanging over her arm and goes toward Wren with it. Wren backs up and blocks her.

"You are not brushing my hair," Wren says.

"Somebody needs to," Star says. She holds the brush out and raises her brow.

Wren turns to the mirror, licks the palm of her hand, and slicks her hair down by dragging her wet hand through her pink-and-blue locks.

"That is so gross," Star says.

Wren grins.

I shake my head and motion for everyone to go. We'll just have to leave Fin. If I wait any longer, I'm going to be late for the funeral, and I simply can't have that. Mrs. Derricks saved my life. She's the reason I'm still alive. And now she's gone. Tears burn my nose and I sniffle.

"Are you all right?" Wren asks quietly as we walk toward the car waiting out front. Our driver gets out and holds the door for us, and we all slide in.

Fine, I sign, holding my five fingers out in front of my chest. All of my sisters know sign language. It was the only way I could talk for a long time. Until Emilio put a pair of drumsticks in my hand one day and I realized I had a voice.

Suddenly, there's a squeal of brakes as a red four-door coupe slams to a stop in the street. The car jumps the curb and lands with one wheel on the sidewalk.

"Sorry I'm late!" Fin yells as she jumps out of the car and runs toward us. She's already dressed, so she just gets into the car. "Were you going to leave without me?" she asks with a huff, settling her black skirt around her as she scoots in the car.

Finch is her name, but we call her Fin. She's perpetually late. Always. For everything.

"Yes," we all say at the same time. We have learned through the years that if we wait for Fin, we'll be waiting forever.

She grumbles something to herself. Then she reaches into her purse and pulls out a brand new pair of gloves. She tosses them to Lark and grins. "Thought you might need those," she says.

"That's why you were late?" Lark asks.

Fin nods, looking down her nose at all of us. "I went to get you black gloves. So sue me."

"You suck so bad," Lark mumbles. She turns away from everyone and pulls her gloves off, and pulls the new ones on. Lark never goes without gloves. Ever. These go all the way up to her elbows and the tips of the fingers are cut out. "Where did you get these?" she asks. "They're comfy."

"At that new shop on Main."

Lark spins her hand in front of her. "Did they have more colors?"

"Only about a bazillion."

"Nice." Lark smiles. She looks at us. "We'll have to forgive her for being late. She was doing a good deed."

"If we have to," Wren grumbles.

Fin flips her the bird.

The car stops in front of the church, and we all get out. We have a security team of two and they'll be with us. Hopefully no one will recognize us, but you never can tell how people are going to react.

Marta and Emilio find us inside the church and come to sit with us. They kiss each of us on the forehead and ask how we're doing. The two of them together—it's like looking at newlyweds all the time. They're so in love with one another that it hurts.

The service starts, and I feel tears prick my eyes and my nose starts to run. Emilio pushes a handkerchief into my hand. I wipe my eyes and try to keep it together. But Mrs. Derricks saved my life. I don't know where I'd be if she hadn't found out about me and made it her mission to help me. I certainly wouldn't have four sisters and two wonderful parents, that's for sure.

The church is bursting at the seams with people, and right before the service is over, we hear the whispers among the crowd. They know who we are, which means there's a good chance we'll get mobbed when we leave here. The security guards keep us close, flanking us on each end as we walk out the door. But when we get outside, there's an even bigger crowd.

Someone inside the church must have alerted social media that Fallen from Zero was in the building, because there's suddenly a mob of teenagers who are blocking the door.

"Oh, shit," Emilio says.

Shit is right. This is awful. We try to speak, say hello, and sign some autographs, but suddenly someone jerks my hair.

"I got some!" I hear a female voice yell as she lifts a lock of my hair, which she just jerked from my head. I press on the offended spot. That hurts like crazy. My sisters start to run when they realize that this crowd is out for blood. I run too. Hell, I already lost a lock of hair. I don't want to lose my clothes. Yes, that does happen.

We're almost to the car when someone's shoe sticks out and trips me. I hit the concrete hard, so hard that my forehead smashes into the sidewalk. Holy hell, that hurts. Someone steps on my wrist, and I scream.

But suddenly the crowd parts, and I see five really big men with tattoos holding back the offenders. "Back the fuck up!" one of them barks at the overzealous fans. I hold my wrist, because it's throbbing like crazy, and roll over onto my back.

"I got you, cupcake," Sam Reed says as he pulls me up off the ground. He moves me around like I'm light as a feather, getting me quickly to my feet.

"Th-thanks," I murmur. Then I realize he just heard me stutter.

"I want to be your knight in shining armor, swoop you up, and carry you the rest of the way, but…" He looks down at the crutches he dropped.

I'd like to see you try, I think. But I don't say it out loud.

His brother picks up his crutches and hands them back to him. Sam looks like he's in pain. "You okay, Sam?" Matt asks. Matt is the one with the long hair and the kind smile.

"I'm okay," Sam says. "Get her in the car, would you?" He jams his crutches under his arms and walks with us, and Matt holds my elbow.

Matt scowls at Sam. "You shouldn't have done that."

"Well, I couldn't just let them walk all over her."

"Um-hmm," he hums. "I think the four of us had it covered, but whatever."

Sam winces as he maneuvers his crutches. *You okay?* I ask. Since Sam can sign, talking with him has always been so easy.

"Fine." He winces again, though, and I can tell he's hurting. His eyes suddenly jerk up to meet mine and he says quietly, "This wasn't how I'd planned on seeing you again, cupcake." He reaches out and touches the side of my face. I close my eyes and take a deep breath.

I hadn't planned on seeing him again at all. Ever. Not after the way we ended things.

"Can I call you?" he asks.

Best if you don't, I sign.

He looks everywhere but at my face for a second. But then his blue eyes meet mine. "Why not?" he asks softly. He stares into my face.

I don't answer. I see that the car door is open and I get in, still holding my wrist. The driver closes the door, and I fall back against the seat.

Emilio and Marta ended up in our car, and I'm glad of it. "M-melio," I say. I try to move my wrist and gasp as pain shoots up my arm.

"What?" Emilio asks. He sits forward.

"I th-think I h-h-hurt my wr-wrist," I finally get out.

He tells the driver to take us to the hospital.

I lay my head back and look out the back window. I can see Sam Reed standing in the street watching the car until it's out of sight. He's standing apart from his brothers and their wives, all by himself.

"I'm glad those boys were there," Emilio says. "I'll have to buy them a beer to say thank you."

Marta clucks her tongue. "They're going to get swamped themselves, if they don't get out of there." The Reeds are local celebrities, ever since their reality TV show started.

I touch the top of my head where I lost a lock of hair.

Marta leans forward and pulls my head down gently so she can look at it. "I think you'll be okay," she says. She pats my hair down flat. She leans close to my ear. "At least your head and your hand will. Not so sure about your heart."

She turns to look back at Sam, but he's a speck in the distance now, and that's how he needs to stay.

Sam

I try not to wince as I hitch my crutches under my arm and make my way back to the sidewalk.

"You hurt yourself, didn't you?" Pete says. He glares at me.

"I'm fine," I say, but my leg hurts like a toothache, and pain shoots through my leg with every beat of my heart.

"Why the fuck did you do that?" Paul asks, shoving Pete out of the way as he comes toward me.

"I couldn't just let them walk all over her," I murmur, more to myself than to him. I saw her go down and I knew I had to get to her. But I don't know how to tell them that.

"Do you need to go to the doctor?" Matt asks.

"No. Let's go back to work."

Matt shakes his head and blows out a breath.

"Did she look hurt to you?" I ask Pete. "She was holding her wrist."

"And she skinned her forehead." He looks at me and shrugs. "You didn't see it?"

"No." If I'd seen it, I would have done more than just help her up. I would have knocked the person who tripped her in the fucking face. I turn to walk back toward the crowd of teenagers but Paul steps in front of me.

"Oh no." He stands there in front of me and it's like going up against a bull. I might try it, if not for the crutches.

"But—"

He points toward the car.

Damn it. I fucking hate it when he acts like he's my father. I fucking love it, too, but still. This isn't a great time for him to do it.

Paul raised me. Well, he raised the four of us. He was barely eighteen when our mom died and our dad left. He took over, and I love him like crazy, but right now I want to trip him and then run from him. Only I can't.

I was in a car accident a couple of months ago, and I broke my tibia, and I got a concussion from a nasty bump on my head. The wreck wasn't my fault. I was in a cab and, in a nutshell, I was just in the wrong place at the wrong time.

My accident and surgery mean that I'm in the city with my family, when I should be playing ball. I play for the New York Skyscrapers, and I got drafted into professional football after college. But right now, I'm benched. And I hate it.

For the first time in quite a while, I feel like a boat without a rudder. Like a balloon without a string. Like a...nobody.

Of course, I can work at Reeds' Tattoo Shop, and I have been. I enjoy it just as much as I used to, but I'd rather be playing ball. By playing ball, I make enough money to take care of things, and I get to do something I really like, even if I don't love it.

We go back to the shop, and Friday looks up from where she's inking a guy's forearm. "Uh oh," she says. "What happened?"

I wince as I sit down, and I pull a bottle of pain pills out of my pocket—pills I try not to ever take—but my leg is hurting like a son of a bitch right now.

"He tried to play knight in shining armor," Pete says with a laugh.

Friday sets her machine to the side. "Who needed saving?"

"No one," I say loudly, talking over Pete, who had just opened his mouth to say Peck's name. I can see the "P" on his lips. "There was a mob outside the funeral home. That's all."

"See," she says, her voice getting louder, "I told you guys you should have taken security."

"They weren't after us." Paul kisses her on the forehead and she tips her face up so he can kiss her for real. He tucks a piece of her hair behind her ear, and she smiles at him. "They were after his girlfriend."

Her brow wrinkles. "Whose girlfriend?"

"Matt's," Pete tosses out. Then he laughs, because everyone knows that Matt would never have a girlfriend. Ever. He's way too in love with his wife.

Friday thinks about it a minute. "Peck was there?"

"Ding-ding-ding!" Pete cries. "Give the girl a cookie!" He scrubs the top of her head as he walks by her.

"That must be why Emilio just called."

I sit up. "What did Emilio want?"

"To invite us all to dinner tomorrow night." She says it casually, but I can see her watching me out of the corner of her eye.

"What did you say?" *Please say yes. Please say yes.*

"I told him we would all be there."

The clamp around my heart eases a little. "You did?"

She nods. Then she holds out her hand so I can give her five. "You're welcome," she says.

I grin. "Thank you."

My brothers go to the back of the shop to get their supplies together. I can't do tats because I just took a pain pill, and that wouldn't be fair to the customers. I don't do sloppy tats. Ever.

I get to my feet and put my crutches under me. "I'm going to go find a bed to crawl into," I say.

"Hopefully, it'll be your own," Paul says, glaring at me.

Of course it'll be my own. I have my eye set on a girl who doesn't want me. But until I'm over her, I'm not even going to try to get her off my mind.

"You going to the apartment?" Paul asks.

I just got an apartment near his and Friday's. They had plenty of room for me in my old room at their place, but I'm too old to live with my parents. Not to mention the fact that there are rugrats climbing the walls twenty-four/seven. You can't even take a nap at their place. It's wonderful when it's wonderful, but it's exhausting when it's exhausting.

I grew up in a big family, so I'm used to the noise. But sometimes I just want to kick back in my boxers and watch some TV without anyone picking on me about the fact that I love cooking shows. And I want to make cupcakes without having to make a hundred of them at a time. I want my own oven and my own bed.

I kiss Friday on the forehead and tell everyone goodbye.

"Why don't you let me drive you?" Paul asks. He's already yanking his keys from his pocket.

"No," I say, and I hobble toward the door. "You have kids to get home to. And Friday to do." I grin at him over my shoulder.

He smiles at her. "I sure hope so," he says. Then he smacks her on the ass.

When the camera crew is here, they eat that shit up. It makes me want to throw up in my mouth a little.

But it makes me envious, too. I want that.

I stick my head back in the door. "What time tomorrow?" I ask.

"Eight," she says.

I nod.

"She might like it if you bring cupcakes," Friday says. She waggles her eyebrows at me.

Peck doesn't like cupcakes. I think she's the only person in the world who doesn't like my cupcakes.

One day, I'm going to get her to eat one. One day.

Peck

I sit out on the fire escape and try to avoid the Reeds and their offspring. I know it's rude of me, but my wrist is hurting like crazy. I didn't break it, but I did sprain it. It's in a splint, and I'm not supposed to use it. I have to wear the splint for a few days and then I just need to rest it.

Imagine that. A drummer who can't use her wrist. The record label we signed with is already having a shit fit. I can't say I blame them. They invested a lot of money in us. More money than I thought I would ever see in a lifetime.

When you come from nothing, you expect nothing. Yes, Emilio and Marta have money, but we have always felt like it's their money, and not our money. Yes, they're our parents, but they instilled in us a sense of discipline and the value of hard work.

I don't need much. I need to know my sisters are taken care of. I need to know Emilio and Marta are all right. And I need to know that my birth mother is nowhere near me.

The door opens behind me, and I turn to look to see who's coming out on the deck. It's almost winter, and it's cold, which means that only smokers end up outside. I don't smoke. But Emilio sneaks outside sometimes when he thinks Marta's not looking.

But it's not Emilio. I lower my feet from where they were resting on the table in front of me.

"Don't get up," Sam says. "I promise not to talk to you."

He gets closer, and then hooks his crutches in one hand, hops two steps on one foot, and drops down heavily into a chair beside me. It's the only other chair out there, so I guess he didn't have a choice but to sit there. Right next to me.

He doesn't say a word.

For a few minutes, he sits quietly, and I get more and more nervous. He grunts and adjusts his leg, propping it on the table.

I pull my drumsticks out of my back pocket and start to tap on the arm of the chair, making a rhythm that matches one of our new songs.

"Did you hurt yourself yesterday?" I ask, my breath billowing in front of us.

"Nah," he says. "It's fine."

I gnaw on my fingernail and try to think of what to say to him. Finally, I just say, "Thank you."

His head jerks up. "For what?" he asks softly.

"For helping us yesterday. You shouldn't have done that."

He heaves a sigh. "You should know by now that I would do just about anything for you."

"Sam..."

"Shh," he says. "Stop making me talk to you. I promised to be quiet."

I can see the flash of his grin in the dark. "You suck."

His gaze jerks to me. "I can, if you want me to."

My heart trips a beat. "Stop that," I whisper.

"Why?" he whispers back.

Sam and I went out a few times, and I really like him a lot. But I'm not like most of the girls he dates, and I know that. I can't compete with them. I'm tall, five-eleven. Six-foot when I wear shoes. Other women are petite. And small. And I'm an Amazon compared to them. But I'm not big compared to him. Not at all. He's six-three. And wide. He's an outside linebacker for the New York Skyscrapers. In fact, when I'm with him, I feel tiny. But I'm not. Not really.

"What's on your mind, cupcake?" he asks. "Spill your guts. You'll feel better."

I doubt it. I shake my head.

"Why won't you return my calls, cupcake?" he asks.

"You said you were going to be quiet," I remind him. *Tap. Tap.*

"I lied."

I laugh. I can't help it.

"So..." he says, drawing out the O so that it lasts forever.

Tap. Tap. "I was really afraid for you when I found out about your car accident," I say. I bite my tongue, because if I keep talking, he's going to drag all my secrets from that place in my heart where I keep them hidden.

"You could have fooled me. You didn't even call."

"I came to the ho—" I catch myself and stop.

"I remember your being at the hospital," he says, sitting up a little.

I nod. "I came." *Tap. Tap.*

"Did I sound stupid when I talked to you?"

He did. But it's what he said that was important. And not what he said to me. "No." *Tap. Tap.* "I didn't stay long."

"Why not?"

"You were busy."

"Busy with what?"

"Busy with someone else."

"Who?" His voice is whipcord strong and fast.

I shrug. "Some girl."

He thinks back and then I see recognition on his face. "Pete said Amanda came by. She's just a friend."

I nod.

"Really, she is."

"It doesn't matter." *Tap. Tap.*

"It does fucking matter!" he whisper-shouts. "We used to date. That's all. She came to check on me. She's a friend."

"You sleep with all your friends?" *Tap. Tap.* Yes, I Googled him. And her. She was a cheerleader for the team. She was gorgeous and petite and all the things I'm not.

"We. Used. To. Date." He says the words slowly. "We don't date anymore."

"It doesn't matter." I try to smile at him. But I can't. It matters. It matters so much.

"You came to see me." I can hear the grin in his voice and it makes my heart skip.

I wish he would shut up.

"God, cupcake," he says. "I wish you wouldn't do that."

"D-do wh-what?" Crap. I forgot to tap.

His eyes narrow.

Tap. Tap. "Do what?" I say again.

He lays a hand over his heart. "You just gave me hope."

I don't say anything, because I can't.

"She was just a friend," he says again.

"Maybe you should tell her that."

"Okay. I will if I ever get in another car accident and almost die and she's nice enough to come and see me."

I close my eyes and breathe.

"I'll send her packing, as soon as I wake up, cupcake." He laughs. "In fact, I'll have my family send her packing before I wake up. Will that work for you?"

"You used to date her." *Tap. Tap.*

"Yep."

"For a long time."

"For a while."

I don't say anything.

"You want to know if I had sex with her, cupcake?" he asks quietly.

"N-no." I bite my lips together.

"Is that why you won't go out with me? Because I'm not a virgin? Because if that's the case, I need to tell Sally Parker that she ruined my life when I was fifteen."

My chest heaves with a sigh.

"I swear to God, cupcake, if I had known my virginity was what you were after, I would never have given it away."

I shake my head. He's teasing me. I can feel the corners of my lips tilting up.

"Don't smile," he says.

I can't help it. I finally grin. "F-fuck you," I say.

He looks at my sticks. "What's up with the sticks, cupcake?"

Tap. Tap. "Nothing."

"Oh, it's something," he says quietly.

I sit forward and rap them on the table, and take a rim shot off the top of his head. I barely tap him. And he laughs.

"So you won't take my calls because…" He stops, prompting me by nudging my knee with his. "Don't tell me it's because you found out I'm not a virgin, because this was before you saw the cheerleader in my hospital room."

I shake my head.

"Was it because of the lights?"

Oh, holy hell. The last time we went out, we were about to get it on, and he wouldn't turn out the lights.

I might as well get this out of the way.

"It was just too intimate," I admit. *Tap. Tap.*

His brows rise. "You were going to let me make love to you, but doing it with the lights on would be too intimate?" His voice rises almost comically. But there's nothing amusing about it. This is serious. Too serious.

"You wouldn't understand."

He puts his bad leg down on the floor and leans forward so that we're almost nose to nose. "So me putting my dick inside you wouldn't be as intimate in the dark?" he asks.

My heart flutters.

"Cupcake, now that I know that, I'm damn glad I didn't fuck you in the dark."

He's angry. I can hear it in his voice. "I didn't mean to offend you." *Tap. Tap.*

He tips my chin up. "If I ever got to have you, I'd want to do it with all the lights on. Because I want to see every part of you." He drags a finger across the upper slope of my breast, and the hairs on my arms stands up. "I want to touch you and see you and feel you and taste you and smell you. And when you make those little noises that come out so much easier than your words do, I want them to be right beside my ear."

He sniffs the spot where my neck meets my shoulder. "Because you smell so fucking good, and you taste better than anything I've ever had in my mouth, and you feel so soft under my fingers." He grabs my hip and squeezes me in his strong grip. "These hips." He groans and slides his hand down my thigh. "And these thighs. Oh, my God," he breathes out. "They're fucking perfect."

I snort. I can't help it.

"You don't believe me?"

I'd like to. I'd really, really like to.

He grabs my hand and pulls it to his lap. "Feel me, cupcake. Dicks don't lie."

I can feel the hard ridge of him behind his zipper, and I press down, because there's a little part of me that wants to believe him.

"Easy," he says. "He's been a little lonely."

"It's not like you're celibate." I blow out a heavy breath through my lips. I'd be stupid to think that.

"There hasn't been anyone for me since I kissed you. Long before my accident, cupcake."

My heart jolts.

Sam sits back quickly when the door opens. Marta calls out, "Dinner's ready!"

I get up and start toward the door. But Sam doesn't come with me. "C-c-coming?" I ask.

"I'll be there in a minute," he says. He looks down at his lap and chuckles. "Dicks don't lie, cupcake. Mine likes you. Almost as much as I do."

I leave him there on the porch and go in the door. "You okay?" Marta asks. I nod my head, and help her put dinner on the table. "You look a little flushed."

"It w-was c-c-c-cold out th-there."

"Didn't look cold to me." She laughs and pats my cheek. "Looked kind of *warm*."

I can't say anything, because Friday and Emily come into the room. Each one has a baby on her hip, and I reach for the tiny one because I need something to do with my hands. I murmur to him. I can talk to babies, because they don't judge me. Not like everyone else does.

Sam

I let myself into my empty apartment and toss my keys onto the granite countertop. I can't get last night off my mind. Sitting there in the dark with her, it was better than any make-out session I've ever had, and I didn't even get to put my mouth on hers.

Peck does things to me that no one has ever done. And she does it without spreading her legs or putting my dick in her mouth. Not that I don't want to do those things, because I do. But she also challenges me. She makes me want to be more. To be different. To be hers. But she doesn't want to be mine.

My phone rings and I see Pete's number pop up.

"Joe's Ho House," I say. "You got the dough, we got the ho. What would you like to plow?"

Silence.

I bite back a laugh.

"Dude," Pete says, "that was so fucked up."

Now I finally laugh. "What do you want?" I ask. I jerk my shoe off my good foot and get a beer from the fridge.

"I'm at Bounce with Edward. Come and join us."

"Why?" I take a swallow of beer.

"Because, man. Edward needs a girlfriend. And every man on the prowl needs a wingman."

"You want me to be Maverick to his Goose?"

"Are you seriously talking *Top Gun* right now?" He laughs. "And he's more like a moose than a goose. Have you seen him lately? That son of a bitch is tall."

When Pete met Edward, he was a gangly youth from the correctional institute. He had bad teeth, a penchant for killing people who harmed his little sister, and he had few prospects. Now he's had a lot of dental work, grew about a foot, and has a good job as a mechanic at a local vehicle repair shop. He's made something of a reputation for himself, just by being reliable and hard-working.

I can't help but ask. "Why can't *you* be his wingman?"

"Because Reagan will fucking kill me. Get your ass down here."

I finish my beer in a few swallows. "Give me a few minutes." I heave a sigh and get to my feet, hitching my crutches under my armpits. The things I do for my brothers.

"Cody and Garrett are here, too."

Cody and Garrett are friends of Paul and Friday, and all the rest of us too. Friday was a surrogate for them when they wanted to have a child.

"What are they doing there?"

He chuckles. "Right now, they're grinding on the dance floor. It's date night."

"Where's Tuesday?" Tuesday is their daughter.

"With Paul and Friday. Where else?"

I swear to God, Paul and Friday should just turn their apartment into a daycare center. "I'm on the way."

He hangs up on me. I hate it when he does that.

***

The music is thumping so loud that the street vibrates with it as I get close to the club. Bounce is the local hang-out, and it's always busy. I used to be a bouncer here and I loved every second of it. I pass by the line waiting to get inside, and bump knuckles with Ford, who is managing the line all by himself. He lets me crutch my way right past him.

I see Pete and Edward, and Edward is talking to a pretty little blonde. She asks him to dance, and he shakes his head. She tries to pull him out onto the floor, but he won't go.

Pete shoves his shoulder and points him in the direction of the dance floor. The dude is never going to get laid if he won't participate in the game. I walk up, introduce myself, and suggest that he buy the pretty lady a drink instead. He blushes, but she nods, all smiles, and he goes to order a fruity drink for her. She looks me up and down and her eyes narrow.

"Aren't you—" she starts, but I put my finger to my lips to shush her.

"I'm just a guy who wants to get a drink." I really don't want anyone to know that I play pro ball. Not tonight.

She nods, but her eyes are bright all of a sudden. She wraps her fingertips around my bicep and squeezes. I lift her hand from my body and put it back at her side. "No thanks," I say.

She huffs.

I point toward Edward. "Go talk to Edward."

"I'd rather talk to you." She bats her heavily coated lashes.

I narrow my eyes at her. "He's available. I'm not."

She lifts her pointer finger and draws a circle on my inner arm. My skin crawls. Edward comes back with her drink, and she reaches to take it from him. I block him and take it myself. I tap a pretty little brunette on the shoulder and say, "My friend here wanted to buy you a drink."

The brunette's cheeks grow rosy and she looks up at Edward from beneath lowered lashes. "Thanks," she says.

Edward looks confused, but he forgets all about the blonde when the brunette sticks out her hand and introduces herself.

The blonde huffs away.

"See?" Pete says. "This is why I needed you."

I shrug. "You could have done that yourself."

I put both my crutches in one hand and hop over to a barstool. Abby, one of my oldest and dearest friends, is behind the counter, so I bang on the bar. Loudly. She looks up at me and scowls. But then she realizes who it is and gets up on her tiptoes to kiss my cheek.

"Long time no see," she chirps. She pours a draft and puts it in front of me. "On the house." Now that I have enough money to buy my own beer, people want to give them to me. I'll never understand that.

Abby is married to Ford, the bouncer at the door. They've been together for a long time.

"How's the leg?" she asks.

"Better." I can't say more than that.

"Hey, are you still baking?" she asks, grinning at me.

"Depends on what you want." I steal a cherry from a bowl on her counter and toss it into my mouth.

"I need about four dozen of those red velvet cupcakes."

"When?"

"Sunday?"

I nod. "I can do it." I've been itching to bake something, anyway.

She kisses my cheek again. "I'll call you." Someone smacks the other end of the bar and she spins around. "If you touch my fucking bar one more time like that…" I can't hear the rest of it. I laugh. I love Abby.

Pete sits down beside me. "Glad you came," he says. He points to the dance floor where Edward is slow-dancing with the brunette. Edward is so awkward that it's almost amusing. But knowing where he came from, it's not. Not at all. He deserves some happiness.

Suddenly, two guys push through the crowd on the dance floor and stumble to a stop in front of us. Cody has his arm around Garrett's shoulders and they're both breathless.

Garrett looks behind them and grimaces. "Is there a really big guy coming up behind us?" he asks me.

"Two of them," I say. And they are big. And angry. "What did you do?"

"Apparently, they were offended by our public display of affection." Garrett and Cody are gay and so in love that it makes my heart skip just watching them together. "Fucking homophobes," Garrett says. He's a little drunk. More like a *lot*. Because he can usually overlook stupid comments.

Pete gets up to cut the guys off before they can say anything more to Garrett and Cody. "I wish Reagan was here. She would kick their asses," he says to me.

Before Pete can get out a word to either of them, one of them takes a swing. But Pete's fast. He's married to Reagan, after all, and

she's a fucking kick-ass ninja fighting machine. He has to be tough to
survive her. Pete ducks, and the blow flies over his head.

I see Edward shoving through the crowd on the dance floor so
he can come to help.

"Be smart, man," I hear Pete warn.

But when alcohol flows, people lose whatever reserve they
might have once had. The idiot swings again, and Pete takes him down,
holding him with a knee on his back. "I'll let you up, man, but you
have to leave my friends alone," Pete says, his chest heaving with
exertion. The guy is huge. But Pete's fast. And strong. And he has good
intentions on his side.

But these guys have friends. "Oh, shit," I breathe, and I pick up
my crutches so I can go help.

I see Edward swing, and suddenly bodies are flying.

It feels like hours later, but I know it's only minutes. The police
push through the front door, and people start to scatter.

"Get out of here," I hear Pete hiss to Edward. Edward is still
on probation. If he gets caught in a fight, even if it was just helping out
his friends, he'll be in violation.

"Give me your shirt," I say, already yanking mine over my
head. "Trade!"

Pete nods at Edward and Edward hooks his elbows in his shirt
and jerks it over his head. We trade, and I put on Edward's bright red
shirt, and he takes my light blue one.

"Give me your hat." I jerk Edward's worn baseball cap down
over my head. "Now get out of here," I hiss. I shove him. "Go!"

Edward backs out of the room, with Abby leading him by the
elbow. He looks at me over his shoulder and I can see the fear in his
eyes as she drags him toward the rear entrance.

"Thanks," Pete says, wiping his brow. The police put him in
cuffs, and his features harden. It's not the first time he's been in cuffs.
But he hoped the last time would actually be the last.

"You would do it for me," I say.

He did do it for me. He took the rap and went to jail for me. He lost two years of his life for me. I'd do just about anything for him.

The police put cuffs on me, too, and I see phones raised snapping pictures. I motion toward my crutches. "I can't walk with these things on."

The officer removes one of them and I follow him to the car. They shove me and Pete into the backseat, and the others go in different cars. At least Edward got away. That's all I can think. That boy deserves a shot.

Paul is going to fucking kill us.

***

They let Pete out of the cell almost as soon as we get here. He works with the juvenile detention center as an advocate, so they know him here. I can see him through the bars having a great time chewing the fat with the officers.

Me—they don't let me out. Not until Sky gets here.

Sky is my brother Matt's wife, and she's my manager. She was an attorney before she met Matt, and she quit to raise their family. The decision was easy for her, since her parents are loaded. She has a trust fund that's worth a lot more than my signing bonus with the Skyscrapers was. I needed an attorney to handle my contracts and to manage my career, and she volunteered.

She has her hair pulled back in a ponytail when she gets to the station. They take me to a room where she's waiting with a stack of papers in front of her.

"They're letting you out," she says.

"How mad is Paul?" I ask. I sink down across from her and drop my head into my hands.

"He'll be pissed when he finds out."

I choke. "You didn't tell him?"

"I did call your coach and the Skyscrapers' PR team. You have a meeting with them next week. And as for Paul, I don't think I'll have to tell him." There's a TV in the corner of the room, hanging on the wall. She points to the screen. "I don't think I'll need to."

There's a picture of me being shoved into a police car, with Pete right beside me on the screen. I wish I could hear it.

But I don't need to hear it, because by the next morning when I get to the shop, Paul is staring at the stack of tabloids in front of him. Apparently, the media has made up its own story. Actually more than one.

Sam Reed arrested for drugs!

I flip to the next one.

Sam Reed purchases prostitute! Caught in the act!

Paul growls.

Skyscrapers' rookie injured in bar brawl!

And the worst one of all:

Skyscraper's cheerleader pregnant with Sam Reed's baby! Lovers quarrel lands him in jail.

Paul opens his mouth, probably ready to ream me a new one. But I don't wait. I hobble out of the shop and hail a taxi. There's only one place I want to be. And it's not here.

I know Peck lives in the same building as Emily and Logan, and since she's not answering her phone, I decide to go to her, instead.

I walk into the lobby of the building and Henry, the doorman, raises a brow at me. "What up?" he says, trying to sound like a thug.

I laugh. "Do you know if Peck's home?" I give him a quick hug. I haven't seen him since the beach, and I miss the old guy.

"She's out with the girls," he says. He narrows his eyes at me. "Did you need her for something?"

"I just need to talk to her." Henry kicks a chair toward me, and I drop down into it.

"Everything okay?"

I nod. But I say, "Not really."

He flips the newspaper in front of him open. "Does this have anything to do with the news?" he asks. He turns it toward me. I'm on the front page.

What bullshit. "They didn't even arrest me. They let me go." I blow out a breath.

"What happened?"

Since he actually took the time to ask, I tell him. He whistles softly. "That's fucked up," he says. "But what's it got to do with Peck?"

"Nothing." I avoid his gaze.

"You're a terrible liar." He chuckles.

"One of the tabloids printed a story…"

"And?" he prompts.

"And they kind of implied that I got a girl pregnant and that it was the cause of the fight. So I wanted to tell Peck about it before she sees it." I duck my head and avoid Henry because sometimes he can look all the way into my soul.

Suddenly, someone pushes through the front door. The smell of liquor precedes her, and her hair is a stringy, unwashed mess. She has last night's mascara blurred beneath her red-rimmed eyes.

She stops at Henry's desk and Henry scoots his chair back. "May I help you?"

"Is this where that rock band lives?" she asks. She can't even look Henry in the eye.

"Who wants to know?" Henry asks.

"I'm the drummer's mother." She raises herself to her full height, which isn't that tall. But she stumbles over her own toe and nearly falls, clutching the edge of the desk.

"Oh, shit," I breathe, just as the door opens and Fallen from Zero comes walking in.

Peck

Today wasn't easy, but now it's done. We had to meet with the label to adjust our tour schedule because of my wrist. They didn't like it, but our dates weren't set in concrete, so they were able to push the tour back by two weeks. They weren't happy with it, but they were able to do it, particularly when we gave them the good news.

It took a lot of begging to get her to agree to it, but Emily is going to tour with us for six weeks. We need her on lead guitar, and with her new single out, she's the perfect person to open for us. She didn't want to do it to begin with, but then Logan—Sam's brother and Emily's husband—agreed to go with her, and they're going to bring the baby. Logan will take care of the baby when she's busy with us, and they'll be nauseatingly perfect the rest of the time.

Watching the two of them together is like watching a fairy tale unfold. It's like turning the pages of a popup book and finding blissful happiness on the last page. They've been like that since they met, and it sometimes makes me wonder if that's possible. But then I remember that people don't stay. Not real people. Perfect is for storybook characters. Not for people like me.

We get home and I stumble to a stop when we get to the foyer of our apartment. Emily and Logan live in the same building, and that's actually how we found it. Emily suggested it.

Henry, our doorman, stands up, and I see a familiar face beside him. My heart skips a beat. But then I smell the woman standing in front of them. I cover my nose and step back. God, she stinks.

Henry motions for us to walk past, and I think that's probably a good idea. But then the woman turns around. Sam gets up and touches her shoulder, and she looks toward him. We slide past them all and walk quickly into the elevator. I stare out the elevator door until it closes, because something about her seems so familiar. She turns to face us and yells just as the door closes.

"Who was that?" Fin asks, scrunching up her nose.

I shrug. "N-no idea." But something tugs at the back of my mind. A memory pushes to the front of my brain. I shake my head, shaking it off like a dog after a bath.

We go into the apartment and I drop my keys onto the side table. But before I can walk away, a knock sounds on the door.

Fin goes and opens it, and steps back with a laugh. "Well, look what the cat dragged in," she says. "I thought you'd be tired after the night you had."

Sam smiles and drags a finger down his nose. "Can I come in?"

She steps back and motions him forward, and he hobbles into the room.

"How'd you get past Henry?" Fin asks.

He grins. "Me and Henry go way back."

I go to the kitchen and get a drink. Sam follows me and I nearly bump into him when I turn around.

"Sorry," he says. He stares into my eyes. "Can we talk?" He looks toward my sisters. "Privately."

My sisters scatter like rats from a sinking ship. Traitors. They all go to their rooms and close their doors. Fin gives me a thumbs-up and grins at me. And Wren makes kissy faces until her door closes. I flip her off.

Sam grins at me. "Watching you with your sisters is like me with my brothers. God, I love them, but they sure can grate on the nerves."

I motion toward the sofa and pull my drumsticks from my back pocket. "Is something wrong?" I ask, as I start to tap on the end table. He watches my hands and his eyes narrow.

He scratches his head. "Well, sort of," he says quietly.

"Is s-someone h-hurt?" I sit forward on the edge of my seat. Then I wince as I realize I spoke without tapping.

"Oh, no," he rushes to say, swiping a hand through the air. "There was a problem last night, and that's what I wanted to talk to you about."

I nod. "Okay." *Tap. Tap.*

He pulls a tabloid sheet from his pocket and lays it down in front of me. I scan it really quickly and my heart nearly stops. "Congratulations?"

The girl he said he wasn't sleeping with is pregnant. With his baby.

"It's not true. That's what I wanted to tell you. I got in a fight last night, but it wasn't my fault and it wasn't over a girl."

"You got arrested?" *Tap. Tap.*

He shakes his head. "No, they took me to the station and then let me go."

"So, when's the baby due?" I finally look into his face. His eyes are clear blue and meet mine with no hesitation.

"There's no baby." He sits forward.

"But the cheerleader." The woman with the perfect figure and the perfect hair and the perfect voice. The one with no stutter and no ass.

"She's not my girlfriend, and to my knowledge, she's not pregnant. And if she was, there's no way it could be mine." He reaches out like he wants to touch me.

I fold up his paper and hand it back to him. "Why are you here, Sam?" I sit back and wait.

"I didn't want you to see that and think...anything." He fidgets.

"Why does it matter what I think?" *Tap. Tap.*

"Because I care what you think."

I shake my head. "What I think doesn't matter."

"It does," he protests. He turns his head and whispers a curse. Then he looks back at me. "It matters to me what you think of me."

"How many other women did you go visit to make this declaration?" I feel bad the moment that comes out of my mouth, but I can't take it back.

He folds the paper and stuffs it into his pocket. "You know what?" he bites out. "Never mind." He gets to his feet and hitches his crutches under his arms. He hops two steps and turns back to me. "Do I matter to you at all?"

My hand shakes as I brush my hair from my face. "What do you mean?"

"Do you care about me at all?" he asks. "Tell me the truth."

"I don't know what you want me to say." I scoot to the edge of the sofa.

"I don't know how you feel," he says quietly.

"We don't even know each other…" I begin. But I don't know how to finish.

"I want to know you." He scrubs a hand down his face. "Do you want to know me?" he asks quietly.

"Sam…"

He hobbles his way toward the door.

"Sam!" I call, because I feel bad, and I feel like something important is about to walk out the door.

"What?" he snaps, turning to face me.

"What do you want from me?"

"I want to take you on some dates." He shrugs. "I want to learn about you, and let you learn about me. I like you. A lot."

"I'm not your kind of girl," I say quietly.

His eyes narrow. "What does that mean?"

I point toward his pocket. "I'm not like…them. I'm just…me." I shrug my shoulders.

He hobbles back toward me and stops when he's right by my face. With him on crutches, I come up to his nose. It's strange meeting a man who's taller than me.

"I like talking to you," he says. He points toward my sticks. "Even when you're tapping, although I'd like to find out what that's all about." He kisses my cheek really quickly, and I can feel it all the way to my toes. I cover my cheek with my hand. His voice goes soft. "I really like kissing you. And I'd like to do it some more."

"But…"

"But every time I call you, you don't answer. When I come to see you, I can't get past the front desk." He throws up his hands. "If you don't want to see me, please say so. I won't like it, but I'll go away."

I want to see him. I want to see him so badly. "Sam…"

He lifts a hand to my cheek. But then his phone rings. "Hey, Henry," he says. He looks at me, his eyes narrowing. "Okay," he says. "I'll tell her." He hangs up his phone. "There's someone downstairs who wants to see you."

"Why did Henry call *you* to tell you that?" Why didn't he call *us*?

"Your security took her out of the building, but she's waiting outside for you."

"Who?"

"That woman who was in the lobby."

"The drunk?" God, she smelled awful.

He nods. "She was someone who once knew you. She wants to reconnect."

She knew me? "Who was it?"

"She said she was your mother."

My knees go weak, I drop my sticks, and I sink onto the sofa. Sam sits down beside me.

"Are you all right?" he asks.

"M-m-m-m—" My mother. I want to say *my mother*, but the words won't come out.

"Sign it," he says, and he lifts my hands from my lap.

My mother was here?

He nods.

What did she want?

"To talk to you."

How did she look? Even after all this time, I still care. I shouldn't care.

"Strung out."

She always was.

"She's sitting outside. They can't make her leave the street. She's waiting for you. Screaming that she'll wait all night."

I drop my head back on the sofa. *I'll leave and go to a hotel.* I can't just stay here and wait for her to invade my life. Trapped like a rat in a cage.

"Come home with me," he says. He looks hopeful, his eyes skittering over my face.

No, I sign. It's a quick slap of my first two fingers and my thumb.

"No one will find you there. If you go to a hotel, the wait staff could rat you out. The paparazzi will be all over the place."

I heave a sigh.

"Come home with me. I have a spare bedroom, and I live alone."

The bedroom doors open, which makes me think my sisters were listening all along. I'm pretty sure of it. "You should go," Star says to me. "You'll be safe there."

I have other choices.

Wren comes around the sofa and puts her hands on my shoulders and squeezes. "You should go," she says.

I can go to Emilio and Marta's, I tell her.

Star shakes her head. "She knows where they live."

I jump to my feet. "H-how d-does sh-she know th-that?"

"She sent them a few letters." Star avoids my eyes.

And no one told me? My hands are flying wildly.

"She was still locked up when she sent the letters." Lark looks guilty.

I can't believe no one told me. How could you do that?

They glare at me. "Did you really want to know?"

That my mother was looking for me? I don't know. I say nothing.

Wren calls downstairs and has Henry tell security to get a car ready. Someone packs a small bag for me with necessities. Then the girls all go down and cause a disturbance so that my mother looks the other way while Sam and I sneak into the car.

We pull away, and I can't keep from turning, trying to get a glimpse of her. But she's watching Lark and the others. She's thin. Even thinner than I remember her being.

Sam reaches across the seat, takes my hand in his and squeezes. I stare out the window, and I don't talk to him, but he doesn't seem to mind. He just holds my hand tightly and doesn't let go.

Sam

She's still trembling when we get to my apartment building. It's not too far from hers, but it's far enough. I lift her hand and press my lips to the back of it, pressing hard, trying to reassure her. She looks at me quickly, and then lowers her eyes, her cheeks pink.

"You okay?" I ask.

She nods, but she doesn't say anything.

The car stops and she doesn't move to get out. "We're here," I say. She shakes her head like she's drawing herself from a trance. She takes in a deep breath.

The driver opens the door and she gets out. She has nothing with her except a small bag of clothes that one of her sisters hastily packed for her. I would take it from her, but I'm on crutches and it's a little difficult to maneuver when I'm unbalanced. She doesn't seem to mind. My doorman opens the door for us and I motion for her to precede me. She looks down at the floor and walks by me.

My insides are at war. This Peck is nothing like the girl who I've seen busting the drums on stage. That girl is fearless. This one is not. And I don't know why.

She leans back against the wall of the elevator and looks everywhere but at me. I find myself at a loss for words for the first time in a very long time. I want to reassure her. I want to tell her everything with her mom will be all right. But I met the woman. It's not all right. And it won't be all right.

I let her into the apartment and she glances quickly around.

"It's not much, but it's home," I say.

The apartment is huge. It's a two-bedroom in a high-rise. It's more than I need. But I wanted some space and it had the kitchen I wanted.

"It's n-nice," she says quietly.

I motion for her to follow me and open the door to the guest bedroom. "This one is yours," I tell her.

She nods and steps into the room.

"The bathroom is down the hall."

Her finger taps on the edge of the footboard. "Thank you," she says. "I feel really bad about putting you out."

"You're not putting me out of anywhere." I jerk a thumb toward my bedroom. "I have a nice, soft bed in my room. It's not like I'm going to be on the couch or anything."

She nods again.

"The housekeeper just came, so I know the sheets are clean." Not that anyone stays in this room anyway.

She sets her bag down on the edge of the bed.

"I'll give you some time to settle in." I turn and hobble my way down the hallway. I hear her door close softly behind me. I'd hoped she would come and join me in the kitchen, but apparently she'd rather be alone.

I go to the kitchen and rummage around in the fridge. I always have a fully stocked fridge. Always. I love food. I love to cook. And I like to have ingredients at hand. I pull out some chicken and everything it will take to make some Chicken Parmigiana. It's simple, but I like it. I wonder if she even eats chicken.

I start to prepare dinner, and she still doesn't come out. She stays in her room. I hear her phone ring a couple of times through the closed door, and when I press my ear against her door I can hear her murmuring softly. Not that I am pressing my ear against her door or anything. Okay, I'm totally pressing my ear against her door.

Suddenly, the door opens, and I nearly fall into the room. I catch myself on the doorjamb. She hops back, surprised. She's carrying a bottle of shampoo and some soap. And she has clothes folded over her arm.

"Sorry," I rush to say. "I wasn't snooping or anything."

Her brow arches, and a smile tips the corners of her lips. *Did you need something?* She's signing again, which must mean she doesn't have anywhere to tap.

Do I need something? Well, I kind of need *her*. I've needed her ever since I met her. But she doesn't need me back.

"Are you hungry?" I blurt out. "Dinner is almost ready."

She glances toward the kitchen. *You cooked?* She looks…amused? Yeah, that's definitely amusement.

"Real men cook," I say defensively, and I stand a little straighter.

You don't have to defend your masculinity, you know? she signs, but she's grinning.

God, she's pretty on a normal day. But when she smiles, she could knock me to my knees if I wasn't held up by crutches. I lean against the doorjamb. "My masculinity is intact, thank you very much," I say.

Her gaze runs slowly up and down my body, and she stops at my most vital parts, her eyes lingering. Did she seriously just do that? Or am I just wishing she would?

Your manhood is safe, she signs. Then her cheeks redden like she just realized what she said, and she looks away.

I laugh, because good God that shit's funny. "I made chicken," I say.

She looks toward the kitchen and then down the hallway. *Do I have time for a quick shower?* She rubs a finger beneath her eye and I can see that she's been crying.

"Yes, of course," I say. I back out of her doorway. "Do you need anything?" I ask as she starts to walk down the hall.

She turns back to me and signs: *Towel?*

I point like she can see them from the hallway. "Under the counter."

Thank you.

Then she disappears into the bathroom. I stand there and listen to the sound of the water as she turns it on. I walk back by her room and stop. There's a wet spot on the ceiling. I'll have to call maintenance about that. Maybe the apartment above mine has a leak.

I hear a tune coming from the bathroom and stop to listen. She sings in the shower? Never would have imagined that. I linger and listen, but then I suddenly feel like a voyeur, even though I can't see shit.

I wish I could see shit. I can just imagine her naked. She's in the shower now, with water sliding down her body, straight down the path where I'd love for my hands to go. Her brown hair is probably pushed back from her face and running down her back like a waterfall. Some of it may be streaming over her shoulders, the ends touching the swells of her breasts…

I glance down. I've gotten hard standing here thinking about her naked. The water turns off, so I scurry like the rat I am back into the kitchen. I can't have her catch me like this, because my jersey shorts don't leave much to the imagination.

I think about steaks and squid and fresh, raw tilapia, trying to get the image of her naked out of my head. I've almost gotten myself under control when she comes back into the room. Well, at least I thought so until I see her.

She has brushed her hair, but it's wet, and her T-shirt is damp where her hair is dripping. I stand there and stare at her for a minute, because I've never seen her in a pair of shorts.

She glances down at her attire and stares at me. *Is this a formal dinner?* she signs.

I shake my head, forcing myself to close my mouth. Her legs are long. Damn, but she's pretty. And curvy. And she's everything I've ever wanted. "A formal dinner?" I ask. "No, why?" I look at the plates I've set on my small countertop, and the glasses filled with ice.

I was thinking I might be underdressed.

I chuckle. "I'd like to see you in a lot less," I say. Oh, fuck. Did I say that out loud? Apparently I did, because her face flushes. "I mean, you're fine." Seriously fine. Like the finest woman I have ever seen. "How tall are you?" I ask.

I hobble with one crutch to the oven, where I had put in some cupcakes to bake before I called her for dinner. I take them out and set them on the counter.

"Five-eleven," she says, as she taps a fingertip on the counter. "AKA way too tall for most men." She laughs, but there's no joy in it.

"You look pretty fucking perfect to me," I say. I let my eyes drop down her body, and her nipples bead into thick pinpoints beneath her shirt. "Are you wearing a bra?"

She looks down and pulls her shirt away from her body. "Yes, why?" she asks.

"Because if you're not, I was going to send you back to your room to get one, because I am not sure I could sit here across from you over dinner knowing you didn't have one on." Might as well be honest, right?

"I'm wearing a bra," she says. "I promise."

I try not to look at her tits, but it's fucking hard. Yeah, that's hard too, so I sit down and motion for her to join me. Her cheeks are pink, and I've never seen anything more beautiful.

I bend over and look at her thighs beneath the table. "God, you're going to kill me," I say. I swipe a hand down my face.

She tugs the length of her shorts down. "What?" she asks.

I grin. "Nothing." *I want to wrap your legs around my neck and eat you for dinner.*

Her eyes narrow. "No, really. What is it?" She's tapping the tabletop the whole time.

"I'm having really inappropriate thoughts about you right now," I blurt out. I close my eyes and take a deep breath. When I open them, she's grinning.

"What kind of inappropriate thoughts?"

"The kind where you're completely naked."

"And what are you wearing?"

I stop, close my eyes, and again take a deep breath. Then I open my eyes and look straight into hers. "You."

Peck

I shouldn't let this happen. I know it's wrong. But it's exciting and forbidden and wonderful. And flattering.

But it can't go anywhere. It's not going to go anywhere. I know that.

I reach for my fork, but my hand shakes. I set it back down.

"We should probably get some things out of the way," I say, wincing as the words come out of my mouth.

"Like dinner?" he says. He fills my plate with food. "Yeah, let's get dinner out of the way." He grins. He jabs his fork toward my plate. "Eat."

"But I feel like there's this *thing* between us."

He nods and takes a bite of his chicken. He chews with one eye closed, and watches me with the other. After he swallows, he says, "There's definitely something between us." He takes another bite of his dinner.

"But..." I sniff the dinner in front of me. My mouth is watering. But I'm afraid to take a bite.

"But what?"

"But while I'm here, I think it's best if you go on with life as normal."

He looks around the room. "This *is* my normal life." He points to his shin. "I'm injured, remember? No training for me. No football." He makes a motion that encompasses his apartment. "This is my life." He reaches over and squeezes my good hand. "I'm really glad you're here. I've been trying to talk to you for weeks."

"Why?" I want to bite it back right away, but can't.

He chokes on his food. "Why what?" he asks when he can finally get a breath.

"Why have you been trying to talk to me?"

"I missed you."

"You don't even know me."

"Whose fault is that?"

I sigh. "Sam…"

He mocks me. "Peck…" He narrows his gaze at me. "What's your real name? And how did you get the name Peck?"

"Emilio gave it to me," I mutter.

I take a bite of the dinner he made and flavor bursts across my tongue. I have to fight to keep from moaning with the simple pleasure of it. "Oh, my gosh, this is amazing," I say. I tap on the table with the fingertips of my bad hand.

He smiles and his cheeks go rosy. So he's sensitive about food? "Glad you like it."

"I don't like it. I *love* it." I take another bite. And another. It's seriously one of the best dishes I have ever had. "Do you cook like this every day?" A girl can hope, right?

He shakes his head. "Only when I have someone to cook for."

"God, if I lived here I'd never be able to keep the weight off."

He grunts. "You could stand to gain a few pounds."

I almost choke on my pasta. "That is so not funny."

"I'm not trying to be funny." He shrugs. "I like curves." He looks down at my thighs and licks his lips. "I like your curves a lot."

"Stop teasing." My heart thumps in my chest like a drum. "If your brothers heard you say that, you'd never live it down."

"My brothers know what kind of girl turns me on."

He looks very serious. But he can't be, can he?

"Is this why you've ignored me? Because you think it's not possible for me to like you as much as I do?" He blows a breath out through his lips, almost like a razzberry. "That's some seriously fucked up reasoning, there." He gets up with his plate and hops to the counter, where he loads it into the dishwasher. Then he leans over and kisses my forehead as he passes by me. He goes to the fridge and takes out a bag of something.

He fits a tip to the end of the bag, and starts to draw circles on the tops of something on the countertop. He's engrossed in his task.

"Why me?" I ask him.

He looks up at me, but only for a second. He goes quickly back to his icing. "Why not you?"

"I'm not like them," I point out.

"Thank God for that," he murmurs.

"No, I mean I'm not at all like them."

"Who's the *them* we're talking about? Cheerleaders?"

"Well…yeah." I look down and am immediately mortified to find that I've completely cleaned my plate.

"I dated the cheerleader because she was nice. Not because she was petite. Personally, I'd whole lot rather kiss a chick your size."

I drop my fork and it clatters loudly onto the plate. Did he really just talk about my height? Right in front of me?

"I don't have to wrench my neck to kiss you. Short petite chicks make big guys like me feel like Neanderthals. I always worry I'm going to break them."

Whereas with me, he'd have to worry about the opposite.

"I want a girl I can hold on to. With a rear end, and tits." His face goes rosy again. "But that's just me."

I'm trying to process his comments. "Rear end and tits," I whisper to myself.

"Rear end and tits," he says again. "Why are you so surprised?"

"It's just…not…what I'm used to."

"What does Peck stand for?" he asks again. He's totally engrossed in his task. But I can tell he's listening intently.

"Woodpecker." I can remember the day I got the name like it was yesterday. "I was twelve, and I lived in a group home."

"How come?"

I shrug. I wish I knew. "My mother wasn't capable of being a parent. Her rights were terminated."

"And Emilio and Marta were looking to adopt?"

I laugh at the thought of that. "God, no. Melio got caught with pot in his car." I snicker when Sam drops his bag of icing. "He had to do community service, so they sent him to the group home. Marta came with him, to keep him out of trouble. She came into our room, while he went to talk to a group of boys.

"She came and sat on the edge of my bed and asked me about my doll. I had been given a doll by Mrs. Derricks, my school counselor. It was the first present I'd gotten in a really long time." I slip further into the memory and my lips tip up in an unbidden grin. "She asked me the doll's name. And that was before I learned to sign, so I couldn't communicate with her. But she didn't mind my silence."

I drop my voice to that of a child.

"'She doesn't talk,' Wren said. Wren was one of the other girls at the group home," I explain to Sam. "Marta admired my doll's dress and asked 'Why not?' 'I don't know,' said Wren. 'I think her lips are broken.'

"Marta leaned close to me. She smelled good. 'Her lips look fine to me,' she said. 'Maybe she just doesn't have anything to say.' I had plenty to say, all right. But no way to say it.

Star—that was another girl— said, 'She stammers. Stutters. Whatever. She talks to me when the monsters try to crawl out from under her bed in the dark. She comes to sleep with me because the monsters think I stink.'"

Sam laughs. "Star didn't believe that, did she?"

"God, no. But she was always trying to protect us. Star was like our mom until she let Marta take over."

"So the five of you shared a room?" He looks up for a second.

"Yeah." I'm lost in those memories for a long moment.

Melio came to the doorway and knocked. "Are you about ready to go?" he asked Marta. He looked down at his wrist. "A jackhole in the boys' room tried to bite me." He rubbed at the area.

"Language," Marta scolded.

Melio rolled his eyes. He pointed at me. "Who's this?"

Marta smiled. "This is my new friend."

"Does she like ice cream?" he asked.

Ice cream. We didn't get ice cream very often. Only for a very special treat. I nodded. I nodded vehemently. But I didn't talk. He didn't seem to mind.

He walked over and held his hand out to me. "Want to go get ice cream with me?"

I nodded again. But I couldn't go without my friends, so I didn't put my hand in his.

"Something wrong?" he said.

I pointed to my friends. They looked almost green with envy.

"You want to take them too?" he asked me.

I nodded.

"Well, come on then," he said mock-sternly. "Ice cream won't wait all day." He gathered his long hair in his fist and tightened the elastic that held it back from his face, and then extended his hand out to me again. This time I put my hand in his, and his fingers closed around mine and I knew I'd found my family.

He took us for ice cream. While we ate our cones, he flipped some cups over on the table and started to tap a rhythm on them. He looked at me and said, "Want to try?"

I carefully climbed up onto my knees on the chair, and banged out the same rhythm he did. He grinned at me. "Well, I'll be damned, Marta. I think we got a drummer here."

He tapped out a different rhythm. I repeated it and he praised me. I was hooked.

I wipe my cheek, which is suddenly wet with tears. I hope Sam doesn't realize I'm crying. I don't think about those days much. They're just still so emotional for me. But Sam wanted to know how I got my name, so I flashed back to that time after we moved in with them, and I remember hearing Emilio with Marta in the kitchen.

"She's like a fucking woodpecker with all that tapping."

Marta slapped his shoulder and he laughed and kissed her. He hugged her against him and asked, "She's all right, isn't she?"

Marta looked up at him and said, "She spoke to me today." I could see the tears shimmering in her eyes from across the room, but I didn't understand why it made her sad.

He froze. "She talked?"

Marta nodded against his chest and he palmed the back of her head, holding her close. "When she taps, she can talk. Something about the rhythm."

"Like Mel Tillis. He stammered, but he could sing. Damndest thing." He shook his head. *But then suddenly he caught me eavesdropping. "I heard you can talk," he yelled at me, but he was grinning.*

I nodded. Didn't say a word.

"You think I'll get to hear it one day?"

I nodded again.

"Whenever you're ready," he said. Then he came and took my hand in his, and we went to bang on his drums.

"…And I've been the Woodpecker ever since," I tell Sam, after relating a shortened version. "Or Peck for short."

"What's your real name?" Sam asks.

"My mom called me Renee. But she also hated my guts. So I'll stick with Peck."

Sam finishes icing the last cupcake and brings it over to me. "For you," he says and smiles at me.

"I can't eat that. Do you know how many calories that is?" I push his hand back.

He waves it in front of my face and it smells divine. I breathe it in and close my eyes. He breaks it in half and shoves half into his mouth. "Sure you don't want to try it?" He taunts me with it. I open my mouth and lean toward it, although I don't intend to actually eat it. But suddenly, my mouth is full of cupcake. And oh my God, it's the best cupcake I have ever had. I moan around it.

Sam's eyes smolder. "Make that noise again," he says quietly, leaning forward until his lips are a hair's-breadth away from mine. I can smell the icing on his breath.

"You got more cupcakes?" I whisper.

"Hell yeah," he says, and he goes to get another cupcake. He breaks it in half and feeds it to me. He starts to shove the other half into his mouth, but I grab his wrist to stop him and I eat the other half too. He watches me closely, and I can see the pulse in his neck speed up.

"Sorry," I murmur around the cupcake in my mouth. But I'm giggling.

"Some day," he says quietly, "do you think you might talk to me without tapping? Just me and you. No pressure."

The whole time we've been talking, I've been tapping the countertop, the back of the chair, or even my toe against the floor. "I...c-c-c-..." I close my eyes and try to squeeze out the word. "Can't."

He grins. "You just did."

I don't know why I did that. I feel like a weight has been lifted from my shoulders after telling Sam about my family and how I got my name. And about my disability.

"You're just being nice," I say, tapping my toe.

He kisses me. It's a quick kiss. It's fast and it startles the shit out of me. Then he finishes cleaning up the kitchen. I try to help him, but he brushes me away. "Want to watch the chefs cook-off show on TV with me?" he asks as he dries his hands with a towel.

I nod, and we go sit on the couch together. He's on one end of the couch and I'm on the other. But this is good. I need this amount of distance, because Sam Reed is going to rip my heart into a million and one pieces. I'm sure of it.

Sam

She's four feet away from me on the other end of the couch, but there might as well be an ocean between us.

I flip channels until I find the chef cook-off show I like. I settle back and lift my foot to rest on the coffee table.

"I love this show," I say and look at her.

"Why aren't you cooking in real life?" she asks. Her thumb beats a rhythm on the edge of the sofa arm.

"I do cook in real life." I point toward the kitchen. Did she forget the meal she just had? I guess it wasn't as good as I thought.

She grins. "I mean professionally. Why don't you have your own restaurant or something?"

"It's just a hobby." I wave a hand through the air, like swiping a chalkboard clean. She just picked up on the one thing I've always wanted to do.

She shakes her head. "It's not just a hobby."

"I don't have time for anything but football." I turn the TV up a little louder and she stops talking about it.

After a few minutes of very awkward silence, she says, "Do you like football?"

I don't look away from the TV. "Love it."

"Really?"

"Yep."

"I don't believe you."

She lifts her feet up onto the couch. Her thighs are plump and perfect and I suddenly want to touch them. I have to fight to keep my hands on my side of the couch, because while she might like me, she's definitely not at the same place I'm at.

"Stop it," she says.

I jerk my eyes back up to her face. "Stop what?"

"Stop staring at my fat."

"I wasn't staring at fat." I look into her eyes. "I was staring at those awesomely gorgeous legs, if you must know."

She rolls her eyes. "Well, stop it."

"Can't. Sorry. They're awesome. And awesome things get stared at. Deal with it." I grin at her. She's not amused.

She puts her feet back down on the floor. "I think I'm going to go to bed."

"Don't go." I grab her as she tries to get up, but with my bum leg, I can't chase her down. I grab her forearm and gently pull her back down, only this time she's on the middle couch cushion. "I'm sorry. I'll stop." I hold up my hands like I'm surrendering to the cops. "I promise."

She settles back against the sofa. "You make me nervous," she admits.

What? "Why?"

"I don't know how to take you."

I shrug. "Just take me at face value, I guess?" I make it sound like a question, but it's not.

"But you have so many faces." She covers her own face with her hands and groans.

"No, I don't." I look at her. Really look at her. "I'm the same guy you see every single time I've been with you."

"I didn't mean to make you angry."

She has been talking to me for about five minutes without tapping or banging anything. I look down at her feet. She's tapping out a rhythm with her bare, pink little toes.

"I'm not angry," I tell her.

"Then what are you?"

"I'm just a guy with a seriously hot chick on his couch watching the chef cook-off show." I lay my hands on my stomach. "My belly is full, my apartment's not empty for the first time in months, and I'm happy you're here. Can you just live with that?"

She nods. She watches TV quietly for a minute. But I can almost smell the gears burning away in her mind.

"Are you going to see your mom? Now that she's looking for you, I mean?"

She heaves a sigh. "I hope not."

"I doubt she's going to give up."

"Oh, I'm sure she won't. But if I wait long enough, she'll do something stupid and end up back in jail." She looks down at my boot. "What's your prognosis with the leg?"

I wiggle my toes. "I go back to the doctor at the end of the week, hopefully to get a walking cast. Then a few more weeks and I can start training again."

"You're going to go back to playing?"

"Of course." I have a contract. "I do like football. Love it." And I'm good at it. "A lot of people would love to be in my shoes."

"Because of the money?"

"And the fame. And the chicks. And the lifestyle."

"But you don't want that?"

I shrug. I don't know if I do or not. "I like to play ball. When I got the contract, the tattoo shop's reality show hadn't started, so it was a way to pay Paul back for everything he's done for us."

I've never said that to anyone.

"But now, he has the show and more money than he knows what to do with, not to mention Friday and the kids. He's set. So are the others. I don't need to take care of them. Or anybody."

"That's good."

I shake my head. "I would like to have somebody to take care of." I cough into my fist. "Someday. Like Paul and Friday. And Logan and Emily. And Matt and Sky. And Pete and Reagan. I want to be a couple."

"You want kids?" She searches my face.

"Yeah." But I don't want them *tomorrow* or anything.

"I'm still undecided about kids," she says quietly.

I nudge her shoulder. "You like kids. I've seen you with PJ and Kit."

"Just because I like them doesn't mean I could raise one." She points to her mouth. Then to her tapping toe. "It might be difficult."

"Raising kids is always difficult," I say with a grin. "Look at Logan and Emily. Emily was terrified one of their kids would inherit her dyslexia." I tilt my head and study Peck. "Is stuttering hereditary?"

She shrugs. "I have no idea. If so, I'm never having kids. Ever." *Note to self: research that tomorrow and never tell her the answer.* "Was it tough for you?"

"Not as tough as the rest of it." She starts to fidget. I should change the subject.

"You want some popcorn?" I tweak her nose and she grins and runs her finger down it.

"I'd have to put it in my pocket." She pats her stomach. "I'm still full from dinner." She waits a beat, blinking her dark eyes at me. "Thanks for letting me hide out here."

I put my arm around her shoulders and squeeze her in a soft hug. "Girl, I've been trying to figure out how to get you here for a long time." I chuckle. "What would you be doing if you were at home?"

Her brow furrows. "I'd be waiting to rate Fin's one-night-stand as she rushes him back out the door."

"Wham bam thank you ma'am?"

She nods and laughs.

"What else?"

"Star would be ironing her clothes for tomorrow."

I nudge her. "I asked what *you* would be doing."

Her face colors. "Nothing."

"Liar." I wait a beat. "What would you be doing?"

"Masturbating and watching reruns of *The Walking Dead*."

Holy shit. I choke on my own spittle. "What?" I finally gasp out.

She laughs. "You asked."

Peck

I should not have said that. I realize it as soon as he chokes. His eyes go all warm and he subtly shifts his junk. I look away, thoroughly embarrassed. "I'm sorry," I whisper.

"Hey, I asked." His attention is all mine. His eyes narrow. "You're lying."

I nod and heat creeps even further up my cheeks. "It's a code word I use with my sisters for eating something I shouldn't." I laugh. That sounds even worse than masturbating because it makes it sound like I have no self-control at all. "You know, forbidden fruits and all that."

He coughs into his fist. "Forbidden fruits?"

"Masturbation. Junk food." I shrug.

He nods slowly. "Masturbation."

I look everywhere but at him.

"Masturbation," he says again. He's still nodding.

"Would you stop saying it?" I hiss.

"That's what food is like for you?" He scrunches up his nose.

"No," I insist. "It's what *junk* food is like. Not real food." I look up at him. "You don't agree?"

"Hell no." He grins. "So tonight, when I fed you that cupcake, we were masturbating together?"

He turns so that he's facing me, with his arm lying across the back of the couch. He brushes my hair back behind my ear.

"Not that I'm complaining," he says with a laugh. "I like masturbating with you."

He tips my face up with a gentle finger under my chin.

"Can I kiss you?"

I shake my head, but his lips are so close to mine that I can feel his breath.

"Why not?" he asks.

I push to the edge of the couch, because I really need to get away from him. If not, I'm going to let him kiss me. And I'm not going to want to stop. But when I move to get up, he wraps an arm around my waist and hauls me back onto his lap. I freeze, because my weight is on his good leg. "S-stop. I'm g-going to h-hurt you." I don't have anywhere to tap.

He says softly but firmly, "I'll let you know if it hurts."

With a gentle push of his hand in the center of my back, he brings me down to lie on his front, and my breasts squash against his hard chest muscles. God, I don't think there's anything soft about him. He palms my hip and hitches me closer and higher, bringing my lips to his.

"A-all of my w-weight is on y-you," I stammer. I close my eyes and take a breath.

"I know, and it's kind of awesome." He smiles. "And so is hearing you talk."

"W-we've b-been t-talking all night."

"Not the same," he whispers. "I'll take what I can get, but I'd rather have you, exactly like this. Except naked, maybe." He chuckles.

I'm already naked. He just doesn't realize it. I put my hands against his chest so I can push back, but he takes my fingers, threads them with his, palm to palm, and holds tight.

"Kiss me."

I shake my head.

"C'mon," he teases.

I want to kiss him. I want to kiss him so bad.

"You know you want to." He grins.

I've kissed him before. Hell, I've passed him a condom before. But we never went any further.

"You've never kissed me. You know that?" He lays his head back against the couch and looks at me from beneath lowered lashes.

"I h-have so," I sputter.

"Nope," he corrects me. "It was always me kissing you."

I'm certain I've kissed him before.

"Kiss me," he says again. He jostles me with a bump of his leg beneath my bottom. "Don't make me beg." He laughs, but it's not funny.

I pull my hands free and take his face in my palms. I stare into his beautiful eyes, and I know he likes me. I am just not sure I'm worthy. I run my nose up and down the side of his, trying to decide if I want to do this. I bring my mouth closer to his, so close that his exhale is my inhale. We're sharing air. I touch my lips to his.

Suddenly, there's a knock at the door. I jerk my eyes toward the door.

"Fuck." He breathes out on a sigh going soft under me, like the air was just let out of the balloon that's his body.

"I'll get it," I say. I push back off of him and get up. My knees are wobbly and I'm sure my cheeks are red.

I look through the peephole and I'm suddenly really happy I didn't kiss him.

I open the door and say, "I think it's for you." I close the door behind her. "I'm going to bed. Good night."

I turn and go into my room, closing the door behind me, although I want more than anything to leave it open so I can hear them. But then again, there's a part of me that doesn't want to hear anything he has to say to the cheerleader. Not a word of it.

Sam

Fuck. I finally get Peck talking to me—with no tapping—and Amanda shows up at my door. Uninvited. I haven't seen her in months. Not since we broke up, aside from her brief visit at the hospital. Peck turns and goes to her room. She closes the door behind her and I sincerely doubt that I'll see her again tonight.

I pull a pillow from behind my back and jam it over my quickly softening hard-on. I motion toward my foot. "Forgive me if I don't get up," I say.

She waves a hand through the air. "No, no, don't trouble yourself." She walks over and bends, quickly kissing my cheek. I have to fight not to wipe it off. "I hope I'm not interrupting anything." She looks toward the guest room and jerks a thumb in that direction. "Who was that?"

"A friend." I try to smile at her, but I'm afraid it probably looks more like I'm gritting my teeth, which is exactly what I'm doing.

"Oh," she says.

I scratch my head. "Did you tell me you were coming over?"

She shakes her head, her gaze avoiding mine.

"How did you get up here?" The doorman should have stopped her.

"Apparently, you forgot to take me off the list."

I'll take care of *that* tomorrow. I swipe a hand down my face. I am suddenly so tired. And I want to go and talk to Peck some more.

I force myself to speak very quietly. "Amanda, why are you here?"

"Do I need a reason?"

"Yes." I say it without even thinking. And I don't want to take it back.

She rolls her eyes. "Honestly, I wanted to talk to you about the photos in the tabloids. Of us."

"Which ones?" The ones that claim I got her pregnant? Or the ones where I hit her? Or the ones where I impregnated an alien and then the alien put the baby inside her?

"The baby ones."

I look at her flat stomach. "Are congratulations in order?"

She heaves a sigh. "Yes."

A tear rolls down her cheek and shocks the hell out of me. "Oh, God, Amanda," I say. I bring my foot down and lean forward. "When? How? Whose is it?"

She flops onto the couch. "Don't worry. It's not yours. And I'm not keeping it."

My insides unclench. Not that I was worried, but for a minute I was seriously worried. "Okay," I say slowly.

"See, the thing is…" She bites her lower lip between her teeth. I used to find that so sexy. But it's not. Not on her. Not now.

"It's Andrew's," I say. It comes out more as a growl.

She nods.

"What do you want me to do?"

"I was hoping maybe you could be my friend." She looks at me, hope shining in her eyes.

"No."

"But—"

"No."

"Would you stop that?"

"No."

"Sam," she whines.

"Does Andrew know?"

"No. Not yet, and I don't want him to find out."

"He's going to be a father, and you don't want him to know?"

She fidgets and I brace myself.

"Well, since the tabloids are already saying it's yours, I thought maybe you could…just…not *un*-say it. Not quite yet. And I'll get it taken care of."

I shake my head firmly. "I am not going to be your baby-daddy. No way in hell. No *fucking* way. Absolutely not." Okay, I probably could have just said *no*.

"Seriously, you're not going to help me? You used to love me."

No, I didn't. I liked her, right up to the minute I found out she was fucking Andrew Tetra. "We broke up. You cheated."

She jumps to her feet and puts her hands on her hips. "You asked me to marry you!" she cries.

"Fuck, no, I did not!" I get up and jam my crutches under my arms.

"Yes, you did! At the hospital, after your accident. I came to see you and you asked me to marry you."

No, I didn't. "You really need to stop smoking the crazy shit while you're pregnant," I tell her. I know she doesn't get high but, right now, she's acting like she just smoked a big one.

"That is not amusing." She lays a hand over her belly. "You did ask me." She lifts her nose in the air, sniffs, and stares me down.

I think back to my hospital stay. I remember seeing my brothers and their wives. And Peck. And that's it. They told me afterward that Amanda was there, but I don't even remember it. "*I did not.*" I point toward the door and hobble over to it, jerking it wide. "You should go." I step back out of her way. "Out."

"I'm not going to deny it when they ask me." She stares me in the eye. "I just want you to know that."

"I'll deny it enough for both of us." I point to the door again.

"Are you seriously going to do this to me?" She folds her arms beneath her breasts.

"I didn't do anything to you," I tell her. "Andrew did. Go see him."

"I don't want Andrew!" she cries.

Peck's door opens and she stands in the opening, staring at the two of us. "Everything okay?" She taps her hand on the doorjamb.

"Mind your own business!" Amanda shrieks.

I stick a finger in my ear and wiggle it around. I didn't know that decibel level existed. Hell, Logan, my deaf brother, could have heard that.

Peck glowers at her and points toward the door. "Need some help?"

"Bitch, just try it," Amanda taunts.

Peck starts toward her, and I have to reach and grab her or there's going to be a lot of hair-pulling and scratching. And I'm out of Band-Aids. I drop one of my crutches and hook my arm around Peck's waist. "Whoa!" I shout. I pull her back and put my body between them. Peck pushes to get around me, and almost knocks me off my feet. "Would you stop it?" I hiss. "She's pregnant. You can't hit her." *No matter how much I want you to.*

Peck freezes. "She's p-p-pregnant?"

"Yes, I'm p-p-pregnant," Amanda mocks.

"That's enough. Get out," I say. The words drop in the room like pebbles on a pond. I can almost see them ripple across the room toward her. They finally hit Amanda and she knows I'm serious. She turns on her heel and leaves. I slam the door behind her.

"She's pregnant?" Peck whispers, her hand tapping the counter.

I nod. "I'm sorry she picked on your stutter." I watch her face.

She slices a hand through the air. "I don't give a shit." I think I hear her say "about that," but I'm not completely sure. "How far along is she?"

"I have no idea."

She nods. "What are you going to do about it?"

I lay a hand on my chest. "*I'm* not going to do anything about it."

She scowls. "Seriously?"

"It's not mine."

She freezes. I see a sudden glimmer in her eye. "Really?" She takes a deep breath.

"Really. That's why she was here. She wanted me to pretend like it is so the father won't know."

"And you said no?"

I scoff. "Of course I said no. Do I look stupid?"

"Well…" She grins and it's so damn cute that I want to kiss her. Right now.

"Amanda's not being very smart about the whole thing."

"If she were any dumber, you'd have to water her."

I laugh. Because that shit's funny. She grins, too. "What were you going to do to her? Before I pulled you back? Yank her hair? You could have broken a nail."

She blows out a breath. "I grew up in foster care. I know how to slap a bitch and make it count."

I grin. "Thanks for coming to my rescue."

"I didn't. I came out to tell you…" She winces. "Never mind."

"What?"

She looks into my eyes. "You *did* ask her to marry you. I was there. I heard you."

"No, I didn't."

"Yes, you did."

I throw my hands up. "Why would I do that?"

"For the same reason you asked me, I'd guess." Her cheeks redden.

Not even close. "I asked you because I fucking *meant* to ask you. I almost died. That makes you see things a little more clearly. When the semi hit the taxi, you were in my fucking head. Just you. You're the one I wanted to marry me. Not anybody else."

"I didn't think you remembered," she says quietly.

"Of course I remember." I brush a lock of hair back from her face and palm her cheek. "I think you need to think about something."

"What?" she whispers.

"When you thought she was pregnant… I saw your face."

"So?" She avoids my eyes.

"So I think you need to give some thought as to why that hit you so hard."

"A helpless child is involved," she says. She clenches her fists.

"That's all it was?"

"Yes."

"Liar."

She turns and goes back to her room. But at the last moment, she comes back, picks up the crutch I dropped, and sticks it in my hand. "Here," she says.

I grin. I can't help it.

She slams the door behind her.

Peck

I close the door behind me—rather forcefully—and lean heavily against it. He wants me to think about it? Seriously? That's all I do is think about it. I made the biggest mistake ever coming here. He offered asylum, but what I wanted was to get a chance to explore what we have together. And now that we've had a chance to explore it, I want to do even more.

I sit down on my bed and flop backward.

My phone rings and jerks me from my wayward thoughts. I grin when I see that it's Emilio.

"What's up, Woody?" he says by way of greeting.

"N-nothing much, Melio," I tell him, using the nickname all us sisters affectionately call him. I can't erase the smile Emilio always brings to my face. He's genuinely good and kind, and he's my dad. My dad by choice, if not by birth, and there's never been any doubt in my mind that he wanted me to be his daughter. Ever.

"If you tell me that Reed boy is up, I'm going to come over there with my baseball bat."

What? Then it hits me. "Eww, Melio. That's disgusting. Don't bring that stuff up."

"I should be telling you not to bring it up," he murmurs, but he's laughing.

I hear him inhale and bolt upright in the bed. "Are you smoking?" I demand. Marta will kill him.

He chuckles. "No." He holds his breath for a second and exhales. "That's my story and I'm sticking to it."

"You're going to be in *so* much trouble."

He laughs.

But Emilio only smokes when something is really bothering him. "What is it?" I ask.

"Your birth mother came by today. The girls say she went to your apartment too."

My gut clenches. "Okay," I say slowly. "Did she say what she wants?"

"She wants money for rehab." He growls.

If I thought she'd really *use* it for rehab, I'd give it to her. "No, she doesn't. She wants to get high."

"I know." He heaves a sigh.

"Should I give it to her?" God knows I have enough.

"If I thought she would actually go to rehab, I'd give to her myself."

He's quiet for a moment.

"There's more, isn't there?"

"She left her contact information."

"And?"

"And the address she gave me is an apartment building that Bone owns."

Everyone knows who Bone is. He's a drug dealer in the neighborhood. He also runs a prostitution ring. And is into all sorts of other criminal activity. "She's staying with a known drug dealer?"

"Looks like it."

"Is she working for him?"

"Define *working*."

"Turning tricks? Selling?" My heart is beating so fast it might fly out of my chest.

"My guess would be yes on both counts. She's pretty desperate."

"I saw her this morning. She looked awful. Does she know where I am?"

"I doubt it. Don't know how she could."

I let out a breath of relief. "What should I do?"

"Well, that's what I wanted to talk to you about." He waits a beat. "Do you want to see her?" he asks me quietly.

Tears fill my eyes and I blink them back. "I don't know."

"She's not the person you once knew."

"Well, the one I did know wasn't very nice to me either."

"If you want to see her, I'll set something up."

It's nice of him to offer, but I just don't know. "Let me think about it."

"Fair enough. How's it going with Mr. Reed?"

"Fine."

He chuckles. "That's all I get? *Fine?*" He laughs out loud. "Seriously?"

"He made me dinner."

I can almost hear his smile through the phone. "Well, that was nice."

"We talked."

"And?"

"Then his old girlfriend showed up, and we didn't talk anymore."

He whistles. "Well, that wasn't what I expected." I hear him inhale and exhale. "Where is he now?"

"Watching TV, I think."

"Let me talk to him."

"Me-li-o," I whine.

"Go get him. I have dad business to discuss with him. You wouldn't understand."

I get up and go to the door. Sam is sitting on the couch watching the end of the cook-off show. He pauses it when I walk up. "Melio wants to talk you. Would you mind?"

He holds out his hand and takes my phone, lifting it gently to his ear. He's wary of my phone. That's funny.

"Yes, sir," I hear him say. Sam's eyes meet mine and I see him grin. I lift my hands in question and he waves me away.

I go and sit down on the other end of the sofa.

"Of course," he says into the phone. He glances in my direction and then quickly away. "You don't have to worry. I'll take care of her."

He laughs. But then I hear a sharp retort through the phone and he sobers, his cheeks growing red. "Yes, sir," he says.

He hands the phone back to me. I lift it to my ear. "What did you do?" I ask Emilio.

"Nada damn thing that didn't need doing." He chuckles. "Love you, kid."

"Love you too, Melio."

"Think about what I asked you."

I nod like he can see me. "I will. I'll let you know."

He says goodbye and hangs up. I sink back against the couch cushion. Sam laughs.

"What's so funny?" I glare at him.

"Nothing." But he's still biting back laughter.

"What did he say to you?"

"You really want to know?" He grabs my foot and jerks it into his lap. My bottom slides across the couch.

I don't think I've ever had a man bodily move me around before. I'm not sure I like it. And I'm not sure I don't like it, either. "What did he say?"

"He said the only thing that could be referenced as a woody around here had better be the Woodpecker. I think he meant you. And that I should worry about castration if I try to get in your pants."

"Oh." What little breath I can get in and out stalls. Sam sort of stole it all with that declaration. "I'm sorry about that." I wince.

"He's your dad." He shrugs. "I respect that."

I nod, because I can't think of anything to say. I lean back and look at the ceiling. Sam tugs on my middle toe. "Did he have news about your mom?"

I nod, and lay my forearm over my eyes.

"H-he s-said she c-came to s-see him."

His fingertips very gently skim up and down the top of my foot. "Did he say what she wants?"

"M-money. Wh-what else?" I realize my tapping stopped when he jerked my foot, and I just stuttered in front of him, over and over. I open my eyes and lift my arm from them, looking down at him. "Wh-

what sh-should I do?" I lay my arm back over my eyes. "Sh-she's l-living with a kn-known d-drug dealer."

"Who?" he rushes to ask.

"His n-name is Bone. Do you kn-know him?"

He stiffens, and his hand tightens on my foot. "I know him."

"I k-kind of w-want to see her," I say quietly.

"Of course you do. It's natural to want a connection. She gave birth to you." His fingers start their gentle sweep again, and the sensation shoots straight to the center of me. "Can I help?"

I shake my head. "I w-want to th-think about it."

"Understandable." He picks up the remote and turns his show back on. "This is the best part." He points at the TV and grins. I lift my feet, but he grabs them and holds tight. "Stay a few minutes. I missed you when you were gone." He grins at me again.

My heart clenches.

His fingers start that slow sweep up and down my foot again. I turn my head so I can watch the TV with him. He talks to the TV while the cook-off is going on, like Emilio does when he's watching sports. It makes me laugh.

He looks at me, his brows raised. "Are you laughing at me?" He grabs my foot tightly and holds it, his other hand holding my middle toe. He gives it a tug and I squeal.

"Let me go!"

He laughs and tugs my toe until it pops. It doesn't hurt. But it's damn aggravating. "That's what you get when you mess with me," he taunts.

I lift my feet from his lap amid his protests, and sit up so I can settle against his side. "This okay?" I ask.

He nods and puts his arm around me.

God, what am I doing?

Sam

Something shoves my shoulder. "Sam!" a voice hisses.

I freeze. Someone's in my room.

"Sam!" the voice hisses again. I look at the clock. It's two in the morning. When I went to bed, I was all alone and I had blue balls from sitting on the couch snuggled up with Peck. *"Sam!"* the voice says again.

"What?" I ask. I roll onto my back and see the outline of a person staring down at me. I reach over and turn on the bedside light.

"Sam, th-there's a d-drip over my b-bed."

"A what?" I'm still not completely awake.

"The c-ceiling is d-dripping water," she says. "C-come and look at it."

What the fuck am I supposed to do about dripping water? Then I remember the growing water stain on the ceiling of her room. "Oh, crap. The water." I should have called maintenance. "How much water are we talking about?" I toss the covers off and grab my crutches. I'll be so glad when I can walk on my leg. I hobble into her room and turn on the light. *Ping. Ping.* There's a steady drip right over where her head should be.

"I th-think it's g-getting worse," she says.

"Would you grab a bowl or something?" I ask her. I reach for the phone on her bedside table and call downstairs.

She comes back and puts the bowl under the leak, but soon there's already two inches of water in the bowl. That's not going to last long.

"Wh-what do we d-do now?"

"Maintenance is on the way," I tell her. I look at her. Finally look at her. She's wearing a T-shirt, and I can see the elastic leg of her panties when she turns. "Why don't you go in my room and wait?" She looks down and flushes.

"Oh, crap," she says. She pulls a drawer open and gets a pair of shorts. I can't draw my eyes away from that perfect round ass. I know, I'm a rude fucker, but I can't look away.

"Damn, that's pretty," I murmur. I bite my cheek, trying to take my mind off it. I'm sitting here in my boxers and nothing else, trying not to let her see how hard I'm getting. While my ceiling leaks on our heads.

She steps into the hallway and puts on her shorts. When she comes back, all that beautiful skin is covered up. Just my luck. Her bra is hanging on the end of the bed. I hook it with my finger and hold it up. "Do you need this?"

She jerks it from my hand and tosses it into a drawer. She slams it shut with her hip. I want to lift her shirt and pull her waistband out so I can see the top edge of her panties, but that would be rude, considering she hasn't invited me to do it, and my ceiling is about to fall in.

I scrub a hand down my face. Now I know she's not wearing a bra. Fuck me. The doorbell rings.

"I'll get it," she says.

A man wearing a one-piece jumpsuit comes into the room, and the building's night manager is following him. She's holding a clipboard and she stops in the doorway, her gaze raking down my body.

Crap. I figured maintenance would come and would be a man. That's what I get for having a gender bias, I guess. The manager's eyes look all over my chest, taking in my tattoos and piercings. I want to cross my arms and block the view, she's being so crass. I hear Peck blow out a breath and she turns and leaves the room.

"I don't know what happened," I start to explain.

The maintenance man is already leaving, though, and he darts out the front door. A few minutes later, I hear pounding on the level above us, and the trickle slows to a drip.

Peck comes back into the room and pushes one of my shirts into my hand. I smile at her and tug it over my head. I should probably

go and get some pants, and if it wasn't the middle of the night, I would
have already done that.

Stomping feet come back down the hallway. The maintenance
guy appears. "The people upstairs have a broken pipe," he says. "I
turned the water off, and I'll get a crew in to clean up the water
tomorrow. We can fix the ceiling, but not for a few days."

The lady is taking notes, and she hands me a work order to
sign. I look down at it. I already took my contacts out, so I can't read it.
"Can you look at that and sign it for me?" I ask Peck.

She narrows her eyes at me in question, but takes it and reads it
really quickly.

"I hope this doesn't inconvenience you too much," the
manager says. She smiles at me. It's full of invitation.

"We'll make do," I say. And then I realize that I don't have
anywhere else for Peck to sleep. Fuck.

Peck signs my name on the paper and hands it back to the
woman. She passes me her business card, and she has written a
personal note on it. Peck intercepts it, reads it, and rips it into two
pieces. Then she lays a hand on my arm, and I can feel her index finger
as it begins to tap.

"Thanks," she says. "But we're all threesome'd out, after the
blonde last week." She looks at me and raises her brow. "Right, dear?"

The workman snickers into his fist, but he covers it when the
manager glowers at him.

Peck presses the torn pieces of paper into the woman's hand.
"Thanks for the offer, though."

The woman leaves in a huff, slamming the front door behind
her. The man high-fives me, laughs out loud, and then he walks out,
too. "See you tomorrow, dude," he calls back over his shoulder as the
door closes.

"What a mess," I say, looking around.

"I'll c-call for a c-car," Peck says. She reaches for her bag.

"What? Why?" I grab the bag and put it behind my back, hanging it from my index finger. "You can't leave." I haven't even had her here for one night.

She motions to the bed. "My b-bed is now a p-pool."

If I could think of one way to get a woman wet in bed, it *wouldn't* be from a leak in the ceiling. I jerk a thumb toward my room. "I have a king bed in my room." I grin at her. "We can share." But inside, my stomach is clenching in terror, because I know she's not ready to have sex with me. Not even close.

She puts her hands on her hips. "I am not s-sleeping with you."

"I'll sleep on the couch." *Just don't go. Stay.*

She looks down at my leg. "I am not p-putting you on the c-couch with a b-bad leg."

"Well, *I'm* not putting *you* on the couch. You're my guest."

"I can just go home—"

"Your birth mother will be there."

She takes a deep breath. "I'll sleep on the couch."

"I won't try to fuck you," I rush to say. "We can sleep in the same bed without…doing…anything else."

She smiles, but her cheeks are warming. I kind of like that. "W-w w —" The word won't come out, and I feel so fucking bad for her when her eyes close. I can almost see the word working around in her mouth. Suddenly her eyes open. "Why?" she says. "Wh-why w-would you d-do that?"

"Honestly?" I ask. I look into her dark eyes. They're so brown they're almost black.

"No, y-you should l-lie to me." She puts her hands on her hips.

"I just got you here," I say honestly. "I've been trying to spend time with you for weeks, and I had a lot of fun with you tonight. I like the way you fit against me when we sit on the couch, and how you laugh at the funny parts of the show I like, and you sometimes laugh at the serious parts. And I like kissing you." I lift my hand and cup the side of her face. She doesn't flinch away. She turns her face into my hand. I touch her bottom lip with the pad of my thumb. Her tongue tentatively touches it, and it shoots straight to the center of me. "I want you to stay."

"D-do you h-have blankets for the c-couch?" she asks.

My heart leaps. She's not leaving. "Hall closet," I say. She walks out into the hall and retrieves a blanket and some sheets, and then she goes out into the living room. I go with her, because there's no fucking way I'm letting her sleep on the couch.

I take the sheet from her and cover the sofa with it. Then I sit down and pat the space beside me. "Wh-what are you d-doing?" she asks.

"Going to sleep." I fluff a pillow behind me and try to get comfortable.

"Go to b-bed," she says. She takes my hand and tries to pull me to my feet.

"Nuh-uh," I mutter. "Paul would kick my ass if I let you sleep on the couch." Paul is my oldest brother, the one who raised us all, and he wouldn't like it. There are some things a man just doesn't do, and letting a girl sleep on the couch is one of them. It's right up there with cheating and lying. "So…" I say slowly. "If you won't sleep in my bed, then we both have to sleep out here." I leave my statement hanging there in the air.

"You suck so bad," she mutters. She didn't even stutter. But I try not to let her know I noticed.

"I know," I agree. "I suck. But I'm a *gentleman* who sucks."

"D-do you p-promise to stay on your side of the b-bed?"

"Does that include errors in rolling over? And flinging arms? Am I going to be penalized for bending my knee?"

A grin teases up the corners of her lips. "You still suck."

"I know." I pat the couch. "So, what's it going to be? Here or there?"

"Fine," she bites out. She hands me my crutches and waits for me to stand up. Then she grabs the blanket and walks toward my bedroom.

In the back of my mind, I think there should be some ominous music playing. Maybe the theme song from *Jeopardy*. Or a doo-doo-doo-doo *Twilight Zone* kind of scary thing. Because I have to admit it—I'm a little afraid.

I turn the covers back and she flips the light off. I hear a rustle of her clothing. "Did you just take something off?" I ask the darkness.

"Sam," she scolds.

I roll onto my side to face her. "What was it?" I whisper.

"Nothing," she hisses back. But I can hear laughter in her voice and I love it.

"You took your shorts off, didn't you?" I say quietly.

"Maybe."

"You did." I wait a beat. Just long enough for silence to settle around the room. "Do you know what that means?"

"It means you should shut up and go to sleep." She giggles. God, that's a pretty sound. She's quiet for a second. "What *does* it mean?" she suddenly asks.

"It means your naked thighs are pressed against my sheets." I groan. I'm turning myself on. Or she's turning me on.

"Sam," she warns. But she's laughing, too. She's so far away from me that I imagine she's going to roll right off the bed.

"You're awfully far away."

"There's a reason for that," she whispers.

"What is it?" I whisper back.

"Because I have this awful feeling that you're going to break my heart," she says. No stutter, so she must have found something to tap on. But I kind of would prefer to think she didn't.

"I don't plan to hurt you." God, she might as well have stabbed me in the gut.

"No one *plans* to hurt anyone else. It just happens. Even to good people. So I'm trying not to let myself like you."

"You like me?"

"I like you a lot. Too much."

"You like me," I sing-song in a playful voice.

"Sam," she says on a heavy breath.

"What?"

"Don't hurt me, okay?"

I can hear the quiver in her voice and tension radiates off of her even from across the bed. It's like a wire pulled taut.

I reach out a hand and feel for her stomach. When I find it, I lift the edge of her shirt and lay my palm on her hip. She squeals when I roll her over and pull her to me. "Sam!" she cries.

I adjust her until her bottom is cradled by my thighs. The scent of her hair tickles my nose, so I brush it out of my face, pushing it down between us. It's silky smooth and she smells so damn good.

"Um, Sam…"

I nuzzle my face into the nape of her neck and press a kiss to her shoulder. "What?"

"You promised to stay on your side of the bed."

"I am on my side of the bed."

She chuckles.

"Go to sleep."

She wiggles her bottom in my lap, and I have to pull back a little and adjust my junk.

"Um…"

"That's just my dick. I told you he likes you. He'll give up in a minute. Go to sleep."

My head is lying on my bicep and I feel her turn her head ever so slightly and press a kiss against the tender skin of my inner arm. Damn, that feels good.

My hand creeps up a little. This is the first time I've touched her naked stomach, and my fingertips are a little greedy. Her hand covers mine and holds it flat against her belly.

"Sorry," I whisper.

She doesn't say anything. She just holds my hand there against her skin, wrapped in hers. After a couple of minutes, she goes soft in my arms. I realize in that moment that I am in serious trouble. Like the awful, terrible, no good, very bad kind. Because I think I'm in love with her.

No. I don't *think* it. I *know* it. What I don't know is whether or not she's capable of loving me back.

Peck

I wake up the next day and immediately realize that I'm alone. I wipe drool from the side of my mouth and roll over. I can hear the shower running in the adjoining bathroom and I know Sam's in there. I wonder if he has somewhere to be today.

Sleeping with Sam...it was different from anyone I've ever slept with before. Not that I've slept with a lot of people. But still. Sam was warm and cuddly and hard and hot and I kept wanting to kiss him in his sleep. I woke up one time to find his hand under my shirt, cupping my naked breast. I was startled, but then I realized he was completely asleep. He held me even when he wasn't awake. I left his hand there. It was nice and comfortable. And I could pretend he was mine while he was asleep.

I roll over and press my face into his pillow. It smells clean and woodsy like he does. I suppose I can't lie in his bed all day, so I toss the covers back. I can hear him talking softly to himself over the noise of the shower. I hear my name, so I step closer to the door. That was definitely my name, in a little chant, repeated over and over. His voice is soft and deep, and a little gravelly.

I push the door open ever so slightly and stick my head inside. The shower door is made of glass, and my heart skips a beat when I realize I can see what he's doing inside. He stands with one hip hitched against the wall, bearing the weight for his bad leg, and one hand pressed hard against the shower wall. His other hand is...busy. Really, really busy.

My heart starts to race, and heat shoots straight to the center of me. I press my legs together to ease some of the ache that has suddenly pressed hard against my clit. It's thumping like mad, and my nipples are aching pinpoints against my shirt.

All I can see is Sam's ass cheeks clenched, so I just have to imagine what's going on with that hand shuttling up and down his dick, and it's a damn fine picture I have in my head.

I should go away. I should let him have this moment, but I'm trapped like a deer in headlights. Particularly when he says my name a little louder, clenches his ass, and groans. His hand shuttles quickly up and down his length until his buttocks relax and he tips his face up to the shower, but he doesn't look satisfied. He looks hungry. His head turns and he catches me watching him.

He closes his eyes and takes a breath, then rinses off quickly. The water shuts off, and I scramble back into the bedroom, because I don't know what to do with myself.

Sam hobbles out on his crutches wearing nothing but a towel cinched around his lean hips. Oh my God, that man is beautifully built. He sits down and uses a second towel to dry his boot, unfastens it to get all the moisture out, then fastens it back.

"You okay?" he asks me.

"Yeah. Why?" I pretend to dig around in my bag.

"I didn't know you were standing there." He's very calm about it.

"I d-didn't mean to…" I don't even know how to say I'm sorry for invading his privacy. I sit down on the edge of the bed. He lies back so that his head is next to my hip.

"Next time, you should come and join me." He looks into my eyes and smiles up at me.

"I…um…" My face must be as red as a tomato. "I shouldn't have stayed. I was just stuck. Sorry."

"Stuck like happy stuck? Or stuck like I-fucking-hate-that-this-guy-is-getting-off-to-thoughts-of-me stuck?"

"Stuck like I-can't-move stuck. That's all. I'm sorry. I didn't mean to embarrass you."

He grins. "I'm not embarrassed." He bends his elbows and rests his hands behind his neck.

"You're not?"

"Fuck no," he says. "I had you in my bed all night long, with my hands all over you. I was so turned on when I woke up I could have driven nails with my dick. If I wanted to be able to walk today, I had to do something."

"Oh." The image of him driving anything with his dick has my clit thumping again and I press my legs together to ease some of the ache.

He catches the move, though, and his eyes narrow. "You're turned on, aren't you?" He rolls to face me, his head on his balanced palm. His free hand draws a circle on my upper thigh. Then I realize that this position has my wide thighs spread even wider. I pull the sheet over me. "What did you do that for?" he whines. But he's grinning. His hand slips beneath the covers and tickles up and down my thigh.

His fingers slide between my thighs, and with a gentle press of his palm, he spreads my thighs a little. I close my hand over his when his knuckle grazes my wet panties. And I am one hundred percent sure they're wet.

He presses his lips against the sheet on my thigh and I can feel the heat of his breath when he says, "I can help you with that."

I jump. "With what?"

"I could make you come. Make you feel better."

My traitorous vagina clenches like it wants to scream *Yes!* But I say, "No, thank you."

He laughs. "I didn't offer you a soda. I offered you an orgasm. No strings. We don't even have to talk about it later. I'll pretend like it never happened."

He tosses the covers over his head and inches forward until he's lying over my lap a little, and his hot breath hits the apex of my thighs. They involuntarily part. Sam adjusts my body like I'm a rag doll, until I have no choice but to lie back. One leg is off the bed, and the other is bent over his legs. He's beneath the covers, so I can't even see him. Or touch him.

"Sam," I protest.

"Shhh," he whispers, but I can hear him chuckling. "You're horny and I want to feel you come. It's a win-win." His palms press my thighs wide and he settles in between, wiggling a little as he positions himself. Then a questing finger edges under the side of my panties. "This will just take a second," he whispers. "Damn, that's pretty," he says.

Then his mouth touches me and the angels start to sing and I totally lose any reservations I had about him doing this. Not that I had many, but still.

His tongue is wicked and marvelous and absolutely skilled. And his fingers…they will not be outdone by his tongue. Not a bit. He licks across my center and sucks my clit between his lips, where his teeth, tongue, and lips do crazy things I never dreamed were possible.

His head is still under the damn blanket, and I have this irrational thought that he's going to suffocate under there, so I grab the edge and toss it to the side. And as soon as I do, I see him. He's between my thighs, his fingers doing crazy things to my vagina as his lips do wonderfully wicked things to my clit, and his blue eyes meet mine.

I come apart, breaking as I thread my fingers into his hair and hold him close to me, coming harder than I have ever come before, by my hand or anyone else's. He doesn't let up as my wits shatter, but his licks, tugs, and pulls grow softer as my orgasm eases. I shiver and quake as he brings me back down. I lie back and close my eyes.

I can't believe I just let him do that. I all but begged for it. And now I'm embarrassed.

Sam eases the edge of my panties, covering me up softly and tenderly, and then he presses a kiss against the fabric. The heat of his breath sets off an aftershock and my body rocks one last time. *God.*

Sam crawls up my body, careful not to squish me, until he's up by my mouth. "That was the hottest fucking thing I've ever seen."

My face fills with heat.

"What's wrong?" His brow furrows.

I look everywhere but at him. "You s-said we wouldn't t-talk about it."

"Oh, crap. I did. I'm sorry." He laughs and shakes his head. "Do you like pancakes?"

I open my eyes. "What?"

He jostles me. "Pancakes. Do you like them?"

"Doesn't everybody like p-pancakes?"

"No. Some people like French toast. Or eggs. Or oatmeal."

"P-pancakes are good."

"I'll make pancakes." He pushes away. But then he suddenly comes back and kisses me. It's long and hard and I can taste myself on his tongue. "Thank you," he says.

I should be thanking him, if I could get my tongue to work. "For what?"

"For trusting me. For trusting me enough to come here with me. For letting me…do nothing we're not supposed to talk about."

"I don't know wh-what you're t-talking about." I sniff. Because we're not supposed to talk about it!

"All I'm going to be able to think about is how you don't taste, and the noises you don't make when you come, and the way you didn't pull my hair or push my face into your pussy." He kisses my cheek and gets up. The towel that was around his hips is loose, and he lets it fall to the side as he gets up. His ass is naked and he turns slightly. His dick is hard and…pierced. I can't take my eyes off it.

"Sorry," I say, jerking my eyes away when he makes a noise.

"You can look at me any time you want, cupcake." He steps into a pair of boxers, grabs his crutches, and hobbles out of the room.

I relax when I think he's gone, and I start to replay all the things that just went on in my head, like a loop. He pops his head back into the room. "If you lie there and think about that thing we didn't just do, you'll worry yourself sick. So go shower and we'll have pancakes and not talk about it." He walks away again. He comes back, kisses me quickly, and says, "Just so you know. That was the best sex I never had."

He leaves. I unclench my fists and get up, and then I go take a shower in the hall bathroom, because that's where all my stuff is.

I can't believe I just let him do that.

Sam

Holy. Fuck.

I wasn't kidding when I said that was the best sex I never had.

I can still taste her on my lips, all sweet and tangy. I swipe a hand over my mouth, but I really don't want to wipe it away. I want to keep it. Hell, I want to do it again.

Watching her come was unlike anything I've ever seen. She's so guarded about her body, and I understand why. Well, sort of. She's so fucking beautiful. She's tall, and curvy, and her dark hair hangs down her back. I've seen her all punked out, and I've seen her with no makeup and no artifice, and I like all the different sides of her. I would like to think that the side I've seen with her here is the real her, the one that she hides from everyone else. I want to think that she's learning to let her guard down with me. I want to think that I've seen parts of her that no one else has seen.

She shaves. Totally naked pussy.

Damn, that was hot.

I'm never, ever going to be able to get rid of this hard-on if I keep thinking about it. But I can't *stop* thinking about it.

So sweet.

So open.

So trusting.

With the lights on.

Talking to me the whole time.

Wet.

Hot.

Tight.

I look down at my boxers, which are tented by my dick. I just came in the shower, and look what she's done to me.

I pull the ingredients for pancakes from the cabinet, make the pancakes, and slice some strawberries to add to her plate.

I can hear her singing in the shower again, and it makes me smile. I put two plates on the table, and warm up some syrup. Then at the last minute, I take out a can of whipped cream. I usually make my own whipped cream, but I'm out of ingredients right now. Mine is better, I have to say.

I spray a circle mound on top of her pancakes, and step back to admire my work. They look perfect.

She walks into the kitchen and her eyes avoid mine. She looks everywhere but at me.

"You okay?" I ask.

She nods.

She doesn't look okay. "Are you sure?"

She nods again and sits down in front of her plate. "Th-this looks really g-good," she says quietly.

A grin tugs at my lips. "Thanks."

She picks up her fork, but she still hasn't even looked at me. Suddenly, she lays it down with a clatter. "You said w-we wouldn't t-talk about it."

"Talk about what?" I can play dumb with the best of them.

She rests her elbows on the table and buries her face in her palms. "*It.*"

"I have no intention of talking about *it.* In fact, I wish you'd change the subject, because you're going to offend my delicate sensibilities." I point to my face. "Is my face red? Blondes blush easily."

"I thought that was r-redheads?"

"Is it?"

Finally, she looks at me. "You're not b-blushing."

"I don't have anything to blush about, because nothing happened."

Suddenly, my front door opens and my brother Pete comes into the room like someone is chasing him.

"Dude, don't you know how to knock?"

He freezes. "Oops. I didn't know you had company." He turns like he's going to leave.

"You might as well stay," I call to him. "You already ruined breakfast."

"I'll stay, but only if you both have clothes on." Amused, I realize he's still looking toward the door.

"We have clothes on, dumbass." I throw a strawberry at his head.

"Are you sure, because I remember that time I came home and you were butt naked on the kitchen counter…"

That was when we were still in high school. I thought I had the apartment to myself for a few minutes. I was wrong. Very wrong. Because all of my brothers came in and caught me with some girl whose name I can't even remember now.

"No one is naked. No one is on the kitchen counter."

Peck's face is flaming red. I hold up my hands like I'm surrendering to the cops to ask for her to forgive me in advance.

"Oh, you made pancakes!" Pete opens my silverware drawer, grabs a fork, and jabs it into my pancakes.

"Hey!" I put out a hand to block him, but I really don't care if he eats them. Hell, he can take them with him if he wants to. In fact, I'd make him a doggie bag if he'd leave. "Why are you here?"

Pete freezes. "Oh, holy shit," he says. I see him looking at Peck. "Dude, I'm so sorry!" he rushes to say. "I didn't know it was *her.*"

"Who the fuck did you think it would be?"

He waves a breezy hand in the air. "Anybody else."

"There is no one else." That comes out as a growl, and I meant for it to.

Peck wipes a drop of syrup from her lip and then licks her finger, and I watch closely. Shit like that makes me squirm when she does it.

Her thumb starts to tap on the tabletop. "Hey, Pete," Peck says.

"Why are you here?" I ask him. He had better have a really good reason for interrupting my perfect morning.

"Paul sent me." He talks around a mouth full of pancakes.
"For?"

"You've got that meeting with the PR people today. I'm going with you. Sky's going to meet us there."

I shake my head. "You are not going with me."

"Yes, I am."

"No, you're not."

"Yes, I am."

"I don't need a babysitter!"

"Yeah, but I'm the one who got you in trouble in the first place." He stops chewing for a second. "If I hadn't called and made you come to the bar, and then if I hadn't gotten in the fight, and you hadn't switched shirts with Edward… It's all my fault. I'm going to go and take all the blame."

"You think my coach gives a fuck what really happened? You think the PR people care if you caused it all?" I point a finger at him. "And you did cause it all, but it was worth it." I grumble the last part. It's true. It was worth it.

"I'm going." He glares at me.

"Don't make me call Reagan."

His face falls. "You wouldn't do that to me."

"I would. I'll tell her to come and get your sorry ass."

Reagan is one of the only people in the world he can't be stubborn with. She always wins. He loves her more than his own life, and everyone knows it.

He has picked up my plate and is holding it below his chin, shoveling the last of my pancakes into his mouth. "Good pancakes," he says.

"I wouldn't know," I reply drolly.

Peck snorts. Damn, that's a pretty sound.

Pete points to her plate. "Are you going to eat those?" he asks her.

She covers her plate with her hand to block his questing fork, but she's smiling.

"So you don't want me to go with you."

I throw up my hands. "Didn't I make that clear?"

"Will you call me when it's over and tell me how it goes?"

"No."

"You will so."

"No, I won't."

"Yes, you will."

I roll my eyes. "I bet your sisters never act like this asshole," I tell Peck.

Tap. Tap. "Are you kidding? They're a lot worse."

"I'm going to use your bathroom," Pete announces. He doesn't wait for permission. He just leaves.

"I'm sorry about that." That's Pete, and I can't explain Pete. I can't even try.

"I like him." She smiles at me. "I like the way you two are with one another."

"Are you as tight with your sisters as I am with my brothers?"

She nods. "Maybe tighter."

I shake my head. "Not possible."

"We were all each other had for a long time."

"Same at our house." Our mom died when we were really young, and we always thought our dad left, but we found out last year he died, too. He died and someone stuffed his dead body into a freezer.

She lays down her fork. "I can't finish this." She puts a hand on her stomach and groans.

I hook her plate with a finger and start to eat her pancakes. If I don't hurry, Pete will come back and I'll have to fight him for them.

I'm shoveling the last bite into my mouth when he walks back into the room.

Peck gets up and clears the table, and then goes down the hallway.

"What's she doing here?" Pete whispers vehemently.

"Eating fucking pancakes!" I hiss back. "Now mind your own business!"

"You are my business, dumbass." He shakes his head. "Seriously, did you bang her?"

"Don't fucking talk about her like she's…less than what she is." I shove his shoulder.

He whistles. "Oh, it's like that, is it?"

"Fuck you. It's been like that for a long time. I really like her."

He opens my fridge and comes back with a container of yogurt. "I already knew you didn't bang her."

"You did not."

"Did so."

"Shut up."

"Want to know how I knew?" He sings it out like a playful song.

"No."

"Because her damp panties are over the shower bar in the guest bathroom instead of in your bathroom. If you'd slept with her, she'd be washing her unmentionables in your sink."

"If they're unmentionables, then why the fuck are you talking about them?"

"What did you two do last night?"

"We watched the cook-off show."

"Oh, hell no." He moans. "You got better game than that! Did I teach you *nothing?*" He throws his hands up.

"Yes, you taught me nothing." I grin at him.

"What happened after the cook-off show?" He watches my face intently.

"Nothing. We went to sleep."

"You didn't fuck her."

"I already told you I didn't, and I told you to stop talking about her like that. Now get the fuck out."

"Did she sleep in your bed?"

I draw in a deep breath through my nose.

"She did. But you didn't fuck her."

He pats my shoulder like I'm a good puppy. "Good boy."

"This one matters," I say quietly.

"I get it." He's serious all of a sudden. Pete may act like a dick, but he's my brother. He's my twin. He's my other half. "This one is special."

"I think she likes me."

"Don't fuck it up by being yourself or anything." He grins and grabs me in a headlock. I can't fight with him while I'm on crutches. He turns me loose and I hop to get my balance. "I have to go. Reagan wasn't feeling well when I left home. I think she ate some bad shrimp."

"Mm-hmm," I hum.

He's oblivious. Completely. "Call me later?" he says. "Tell me how it goes with the PR people?"

I nod. "I'll think about it."

He goes toward the door, stops, and flashes me the *I love you* sign. "Love you, dumbass," he says. Then he leaves. I should have gotten his key. That would have been smart.

Peck comes out of her room and she's carrying her purse. She's dressed in a pair of jeans and a T-shirt, and she has makeup on. She's so pretty. "Did Pete leave?" she asks.

"He had to go hold Reagan's hair back while she pukes."

"Eww." She wrinkles her nose.

"I'm pretty sure she's pregnant."

Her face softens. "Oh," she breathes out in a happy sigh.

"Pete doesn't know it yet." I laugh. I like knowing something he doesn't know.

"Are you sure?"

I shake my head. "No. But they stopped using condoms when they got married, so one plus one must equal two. Or three, as the case may be."

"So, you guys t-talk about that stuff?" she asks. Her voice goes quiet, and she suddenly looks nervous.

I shrug. "Some of it."

"Did you talk about m-me?" She's almost whispering.

I walk close enough that my chest brushes hers. I push her hair back behind her ear. "We talked about you."

Her eyes jerk up to meet mine. "You told him about this morning?"

She is flustered all of a sudden, so I feel the intense need to comfort her. "Nothing happened this morning." Nothing that didn't rock my world. "I wouldn't talk with him about that."

"But you talk about everything." Her hand lands on my chest, like she needs to steady herself.

"I want to hold that close to my heart. Well, that thing we *didn't do*, I want to keep it to myself."

"You really didn't tell him?" She looks hopeful.

I shake my head. "I told him how much I like you."

She smiles.

"Do you like me back?"

She nods. "I do," she whispers. "Lots."

"I remember when my brothers found the women they were supposed to be with. The moment they met them, they treasured them, their relationship, and the bond between them above all else. We talk, but we don't cross any lines. I value you. I want you to know how much. I didn't talk about anything we did together. Nothing." I lift the edge of her shirt so I can settle my hands on her naked waist, but she pushes my hands away. "What's wrong?"

"I can't get used to all the touching you do. It's strange. And makes me feel vulnerable, because my body is far from perfect."

It took a lot for her to say that, I can tell. She's worried about me touching a pudgy spot? Seriously? I live for pudge. Bring it on. "You want me to keep my hands to myself?"

She shakes her head. "No."

I kiss the tip of her nose. She scrunches up her face, and then brackets my face with her hands, looks into my eyes, and kisses me. Damn, she really kisses me. Her tongue touches mine and I'm almost lost, but then she pulls back and looks at her watch. "I have to go to the studio to meet the Zeroes."

"Are you coming back tonight?" I try not to sound too hopeful, but damn it, I am.

She's startled. "You don't want me to?"

"I want you here every fucking day, cupcake. All the time."

She smiles. "Okay," she whispers. "I have a car waiting outside with a driver. I had better go."

I take a key from my junk drawer and press it into her hand. "In case I'm not back yet."

"I hope everything goes okay with the team," she says. Then she slips out the door.

And that's when I realize that ever since she came out of the bathroom, she didn't tap one single time, not even her toes, and she didn't stutter even the first time. That makes me feel all gooey inside. Gooey and melty and needy.

God, she's going to make me need her, and then she's going to walk away. I can tell.

***

When I get to the Skyscrapers' office, Sky is waiting out front for me. She has on a business suit, and her hair is in a knot on top of her head. She's leaning on her hip against a streetlight, the soft swell of her belly evident. "You're looking a little pregnant, there," I tell her.

She smoothes her hand down her stomach. "I know, right? I don't remember being this big the last time I was five months pregnant, and I had two of them in there."

We thought Matt would never be able to have kids, not after the chemo, but now he has five and one on the way. He's going for a softball team.

I kiss her on the forehead. "How are you feeling?"

"Oh, this is the easy part." She smiles up at me. "How are you?"

Well, I had Peck in my bed when I woke up, and then she came on my face, and then we had pancakes together. "Great."

"And Peck?" She narrows her eyes at me.

"What about her?"

She opens the door so I can hobble my way through it. "How is she?"

I shrug. "Fine, I guess."

She shoves my shoulder and almost knocks me off my crutches. "Don't be evasive with me. We all know she spent the night with you last night."

I raise my brows at her. "You want me to give you all the details?"

Her cheeks get rosy. "I'll leave that to your brothers." She glares at me. "She's okay, though, right?"

"She's fine." I reach out to scrub her hair but she ducks and avoids me. Sky is getting way too good at this being-a-Reed thing.

"And you? Are you all right?"

"Why wouldn't I be?"

"Just checking."

We step into the outer office and the receptionist motions us into a room where my coach, some PR people, the general manager, and the team lawyer are all waiting. I'm suddenly a little intimidated.

"How's the leg?" Coach asks.

"Getting better," I say. "I'm anxious to get this thing off and get back to playing."

He smiles at me and nods. "We want the same thing you do. But we have some things to discuss." He motions the team lawyer and the PR people forward, and a man shows me all the news clippings and false accusations that have been floating around. There are a lot more than I even knew about.

The lawyer takes out a pen and a piece of paper. "What happened the night you got arrested?"

"I went to meet my brother and one of his friends at Bounce, and two of our good friends happened to be there." I point to the picture. "The men in question didn't approve of their relationship, and my friends were being harassed by them. We told the bullies to cool it, and they started swinging. That's all it was. We were defending ourselves."

Sky says, "Sam is aware of the consequences of his actions, and since he already has a solid presence in the community, we feel like dealing with this publicly has been punishment enough."

The lawyer sits back. "We'll decide what's punishment enough."

Sky continues like he didn't say a word. She lays photos on the desk. I've never even seen these. "These are some of the causes Sam's already involved in." She points to them one by one. "Raising money for the homeless shelters in the city." She points to another. "Assisting with the youth program at the juvenile detention center." She throws about ten more onto the table. "I've already leaked these to the media. We should see the outlets start to pick them up in the next day or two." She sits back and crosses her legs. "So as you can see, gentlemen, Sam is and will continue to be an upstanding member of the community." She blinks her eyes at me, prompting me to contribute.

"I plan to continue to serve the community, and hopefully we can put this whole mess behind us. I sincerely regret any problems my actions caused for the organization, my teammates, and my coaches."

Sky smiles at me and winks.

The lawyer looks wolfishly at her. I think he realizes he's just been bested. "There's another matter," he says. He shoves a picture of Amanda toward me. "A child?"

Sky's eyes jerk to meet mine.

"It's not mine," I rush to say.

"Are you certain?" the lawyer asks.

"I believe I'd know if I had sex with her, sir. Recently, I mean. Our relationship has been over for months. That baby is not mine."

"You'll be asked to take a paternity test."

"Gladly."

The man scribbles in his notebook. "Do you currently have a girlfriend, Sam?" he asks.

"I don't believe—" Sky starts.

But I cut her off. "Yes, I do."

"What's her name?" He taps his pen against his notepad.

I look at Sky. She nods.

"Her name is Peck Vasquez."

"How long have you been dating?"

Since last night. "A few months." Well, that's true if you count the time we spent together before. And there hasn't been anyone else for me since the day I met her.

"You'll want to be seen with her in public to mitigate the damage caused by Amanda's allegations."

"Not a problem." I'd go anywhere with Peck.

Suddenly, he stands up and sticks out his hand. I take it and give it a shake. "It was nice meeting you." He looks at Sky. "Mrs. Reed, I'll send over a list of suggested actions for your review."

Sky nods and he leaves the room. The coach claps me on the shoulder. "We'll need for you to see the team doctor. He's waiting for you in the training room. We look forward to having you back out on the field as soon as possible."

He looks down at his watch, curses softly, makes his excuses and leaves with the PR people, all of whom are going to send notes to Sky about further positive actions.

When the room is empty, I look at her and grin. "You totally rocked that," I tell her.

She shrugs. "All in a day's work." But she's grinning too. "I can't believe they didn't even fine you."

"Well, when you think about it, I didn't do anything wrong."

"Do you need me to go with you to see the trainer?" she asks as she packs up her things.

"I can handle it," I tell her. "Thanks for making it all work out."

"Matt helped me with it," she says sheepishly.

"You two make one hell of a team."

She laughs. "I know." She kisses me on the cheek and leaves. I sit back and scrub a hand down my face. That could have gone so differently.

I go and meet with the trainer. The best part of the day— getting a walking boot so I can ditch the crutches. I step gingerly onto my foot. It's not completely comfortable, but I'll get used to it. Anything would be better than the crutches. The trainer gives me a schedule for physical therapy, and I have to start weight training with my arms and upper body right away. Football is a demanding sport. I want to be in shape when I go back onto the field, so I don't complain a bit.

I go home with thoughts of Peck on my mind. A celebration is in order, so I stop and buy things to cook for dinner, and the right ingredients for dessert. I love having someone to cook for. I like taking care of her. And I can't wait to see her again.

Peck

A paper clip bounces off the side of my head, and I jump.
Wren waves at me from across the room. "Earth to Peck," she chants.
She throws up her hands in question. "What is up with you?"

"She's thinking about Sam Reed's dick," Fin says over a laugh. I
throw the paperclip at her and she lifts her hands to deflect it.

"I was n-not thinking about Sam's dick," I mumble. I *might*
have been thinking about his tongue. Or maybe his fingers. But I
wasn't thinking about his dick—not until Fin mentioned it, at least.

"Hey," I whisper to Fin. "Have you ever slept w-with a guy
who has a piercing?"

"Sam has his dick pierced?" she says really loudly. She cups a
hand around her ear like she's a little old lady with an ear trumpet for
better hearing. "Did I hear you right?"

"Would you shut up?" I grumble. But I'm laughing too. I can't
help it.

We're at the recording studio so that we can record some new
vocals for one of the songs on our upcoming album. They weren't
quite perfect. We're waiting for the guy who runs the board to get here.

My sisters were spread out around the room, but now they all
head in my direction.

"So Sam is pierced, huh?" Wren asks. She grins. "Figures you
would get the good Reed."

"She got the last Reed left," Lark pretends to grumble.

"I think they're all pierced, so it's a moot point." Fin grins and
waggles her brows.

"How would you know?" Wren pretends to be offended by the
fact that Fin might know something the rest of us don't.

"Emily told me." She shrugs. "But it does suck that you got the
last Reed."

"There's still Seth," Fin reminds us all.

"True," Wren says. "And he's hot. Even though he's not a
blond." He's like the opposite of blond, with his swarthy good looks.

I'm pretty sure his mom was half black and half white, and his dad was Latino, so he has a mass of dark, silky, curly hair and eyes the color of fall. He's handsome, and on top of all that, he's funny and charming. And hot. "He's too young, though."

"He's the same age you are," I remind Wren.

"He seems so much younger," Wren replies.

"So about that piercing..." Fin says. She laughs and rubs her hands together like she's chafing them. "Tell us more."

Heat creeps up my cheeks. "I don't know anything about a piercing." I'm a bad liar, and they all know it.

"You slept with him," Fin says, deadpan.

"Well..." I hedge.

"Oh, shut the fuck up," Wren breathes. "You did Sam Reed?"

"No, I didn't do him." I let my voice drop down really low. "He kind of did me."

All my sisters' eyebrows rise and their mouths fall open. Fin points rather obscenely toward her crotch. "He took it downtown? Ate at the Y? Had a box lunch?"

I don't answer, but the heat on my face must tell the story well, because Fin slaps her thighs and starts to laugh.

"I knew that boy would be good. Can I have him when you're finished with him?"

"I'm not going to f-finish with him." I pick up a stapler and pretend to fix it, even though I'm pretty sure there's nothing wrong with it.

"So, how was it?" Fin asks.

"Good," I squeak.

Fin is the one who has all the one-nighters, and she's not afraid to talk about sex in any way, shape, or form. Star is the prude, and she's glaring at us from across the room with a frown on her face. I pull Fin to the side so only she can hear me.

"So, tell me what you do with it," I whisper.

"Do with what? It's a dick. You plant it. You water it. You watch it grow. Maybe not in that order."

"I know what to do with a dick. But what do you do with a piercing?"

"Let it pleasure you. That's about it." She steals my bag of popcorn and pops a piece into her mouth.

"So you don't, like, have to do anything with it?"

"Nope. You might lick around it or something. But even that's not necessary. It's for aesthetics more than anything. And the naughty factor." She narrows her eyes. "So, did you get off?"

"Um…yep. Quickly." I blow out a breath. Really quickly. "Mad skills."

"And how did you feel after?"

"What do you mean?"

"Did you feel used? Pressured? Pushed? Uncomfortable?"

"God, no. He was really sweet." I smile at the thought of how he touched me. Softly, but firmly. Reverently. Respectfully.

"Then what's your problem?"

"What makes you think I have a problem?"

Her left brow rises. "Because you always have problems in the sack. Although I'm still not sure why."

Fin is just about the opposite of me. She's short and blonde and fun-sized. Emilio used to call her Snickers and joked that he could put her in his pocket.

"I would kill for a body like yours," Fin says.

We always want what we don't have, don't we? Fin is perfect to me, and yet even she would change her body.

"So, let's talk about sex," she says. "Is there anything you want to know? Talk to me, kiddo."

I laugh. "I think I'm okay. Just never had a piercing before. Wasn't sure what to do with it."

"You really like him." She doesn't ask it as a question. It's just a statement.

"Yeah, I do."

"What about what happened at the hospital? The night he professed his undying love for you and then asked some hooch to marry him."

"He was on pain meds." Should I tell her? Hell, I need to tell someone. "The hooch came to see him last night. She's pregnant."

"Who's pregnant?" Star calls from across the room.

I lay my head back and groan. "Good grief," I say. Then I tell them all what happened last night, with the girl showing up and the ceiling falling in.

"Well, that's a fine way to get a woman into your bed," Star says over a sniff. "Have a ceiling drop on her. That seems like overkill, though."

"Do you want me to get a hotel room with you tonight?" Lark asks. "I'd do that for you."

I know she would, but I kind of want to go back to Sam's. I like the way this feels, and I really want to see where it's going to go. "I'm okay with Sam."

"Bow-chick-a-wow-wow," Fin sings out. "I want details about that piercing."

The owner of the studio we're using comes into the room. Star claps her hands together like a teacher. "We really need to get back to work, ladies," she says.

When the others trickle off, Star turns to me. "You're being smart, right?"

I nod. As smart as I can be.

"Use a condom. Those Reed men breed like rabbits." Then she walks into the booth with the others and we get set up to record some vocals.

Rabbits. Little Reeds. I have to say, that's not an entirely bad thought.

Sam

It's really nice walking on both feet for a change. My leg is still a bit sore, and I know I'm hobbling a little, but just about anything would be better than crutches.

I walk into the tattoo shop and am surprised to find that three of my brothers are there. They usually space it out so that they don't all have to work at the same time. Since they expanded the shop, added more stations, and hired a few more artists, the place is busy all the time. That probably has something to do with the reality TV show about us, but still.

Logan sets his machine to the side. *Nice,* he signs, pointing to my leg.

"I know, right?" I sit down in a chair with wheels and spin it around in a slow circle. "It's a lot less heavy."

Paul picks up the schedule clipboard. "You're not working today, are you?" He sets the clipboard to the side.

I shake my head. "Pete called and said he wanted to have a family meeting. Told me to meet him here."

"Oh, fuck," Paul swears. "What did he do now?"

I shrug. No telling with Pete.

"Everything go okay with the team this morning?" Matt asks, but he's grinning, so I'm sure that Sky already told him what happened.

"Your wife is amazing," I tell him with a smile.

"I know," he brags. "You should see her in the sack."

"Eww," Logan says.

All my brothers sign while they talk so Logan doesn't miss anything. It's habit. He doesn't catch everything reading lips, so we all learned to sign early on. It's second nature to us.

Paul throws a rag at Matt. "Dude, don't talk shit about my sister-in-law."

Matt laughs and throws it back at him.

The door opens and Pete walks in. He jams his hands in his jeans pockets and rocks back and forth from his heels to his toes. "Do you guys have time to talk?" he asks.

Paul gets up and waves a hand toward the back of the shop. There's an office in the rear of the shop and we go there when we want privacy. It's the only place in the building with no cameras.

Paul closes the door once we're all inside. He turns to Pete. "Let me guess. Reagan's pregnant and you're scared shitless," he deadpans.

All the blood drains from Pete's face. "What? Reagan's pregnant?" He looks at each of us in turn.

"Oh, fuck," Paul says. "You didn't know."

"How the fuck did you know and I didn't?" Pete says, his voice rising.

"We didn't know," Matt says. "He was just guessing, because all of us, aside from Sam, came to him when we had one on the way." Matt glares at Paul. "Why did you have to go and ruin it?"

"Hell, I thought everyone knew. She's been sick for the past week."

"Bad shrimp," Pete says.

"Bad shrimp wouldn't make her throw up *every* morning," Logan chimes in. He can speak when he wants to. "She's knocked up."

Pete sinks down in a chair like his legs have turned to noodles.

Logan raises his hand. "When I suspected Em was pregnant and I came to spill my guts to Paul, it was because Em's boobs were getting bigger."

"Sky's did too," Matt chimes in.

Paul nods. "Same here."

Pete looks around the room. "Reagan's boobs *are* bigger, and she's sick every morning. And afternoon. Hell, even in the evening." He smiles, and I imagine I can see stars floating in the air around his head. "I'm going to be a dad?"

"Sorry we ruined the surprise. We've had bets going for a whole week to find out if you'd realize it before Reagan does." Matt shrugs.

"One of you could have told me!" Pete cries. But he's grinning like a damn fool. He points around the room at each of us. "So, which of you bet Reagan would know first?"

I raise my hand. I figured she's the one with the uterus, so she'd realize it before Pete did.

"You lost, little brother," Paul says. He walks by me and squeezes my shoulder.

"Doesn't count if you tell him," I complain.

Paul wraps his beefy arm around Pete's head and gives him a noogie. Pete's still in la-la land though, so he doesn't even struggle.

"Stop and get a test on the way home," Matt tells him.

"Okay." Pete's still star-struck.

"Wait," I say. "If you didn't want to tell us Reagan's pregnant, what did you call me here for?"

Pete throws up his hands. "Hell, I can't remember." He stares into space for a minute with a goofy grin on his face, until he suddenly slaps his thigh. "Oh, I remember now." He winces. "I have this man from the correctional facility..." He waits, watching our faces. But if we had a nickel for every time Pete says this, we'd be rich men.

"What does he need?" Paul asks.

"He needs a job."

"Violent crime?" Paul asks.

"Gang-related."

"Is he out?" Matt wants to know.

Pete nods. "He's all the way out. But now he's having trouble finding a job. This guy has so much potential. I don't want to see him get lost in the system."

"How old?"

"Twenty-seven?"

We're all startled. Pete usually brings us juveniles he wants us to big-brother. Not adults.

"He'll do anything," Pete rushes to say. "He just needs a chance. And he's an amazing artist."

"So have him bring some art samples in," Paul says.

"He's out in my car, and he has samples with him. Sort of."

Paul's eyes narrow. "So bring him in."

We all go back out to the main area and Pete walks outside. Then the door jingles a few minutes later when he comes back in. I've seen Pete with some shady-looking characters, but I've never seen anyone like this guy. He has a tattoo on the side of his face. It's a cluster of teardrops. In our neighborhood, tattoos like that are usually gang-related and it means he's killed someone. He has more than one teardrop.

But what's even more surprising is that he's on wheels.

Paul walks up to him and sticks out his hand. "Paul Reed," he says. He introduces us all.

"Nice to meet you," the man says. "My name is Joshua. Friends just call me Josh." He shakes hands with each of us.

"Pete said you had some art samples," Paul says.

"Oh yeah," he says quickly, and he reaches back and pulls his shirt over his head the way guys do.

The guy is covered in ink. But when you look closely, you can tell it wasn't done by traditional machines. It's prison ink. But it's fucking beautiful.

"Nice," I say. I look at my brothers. I shrug. I'm impressed. I can't help it.

He pulls his shirt back on. "I lost the use of my legs, and with my felony record, it's not easy to find a job. Pete said you might need some help."

"I can't put you doing tats," Paul says.

"Oh, I understand," Joshua rushes to say. "I'll do anything."

"Give us a minute to talk it over," Paul says, and we all follow him back to the office.

"He just needs a chance," Pete says.

"Will anyone be coming for him?"

"I don't think so."

Paul nods. "Show of hands? Yes?"

None of us raise a hand.

"He needs to be somewhere that no one will see the chair," Pete says. "He needs to learn it doesn't define him."

"Is he always nice?" Matt asks.

"No," Pete says. "Sometimes he's normal." He laughs. "Just give him a chance. If you want, you can set it up so that he's only here when I'm here."

"You're in charge of him," Paul says.

"Okay." Pete takes a breath. "So you'll give him a shot?"

"Only when you're here," Paul says. "Where's he living?"

"Transitional housing."

I snort. I figured he would have been staying with Pete.

"I couldn't take Josh home to Reagan. She'd beat the shit out of him if he flinches. He's not like the kids I take home. He's a man. A man who needs a second chance." Pete looks hopeful.

Paul blows out a breath and walks back out to the front of the shop. "Josh, get with Pete about a schedule. If you want to stay today, you can start by sweeping, taking the trash out, and you can clean out the fridge."

Josh looks wary, instead of joyful like I would have expected. "Yes, sir," he says.

"Don't call me sir," Paul says. "Just Paul will do."

"Where can I find cleaning supplies?" Josh asks.

Pete walks him back to the supply closet, chattering like he's a tour director.

"You sure this is a good idea?" I ask Paul.

"No." He slams the cabinet door where he's pulled out a bottle of ink.

"You can put him on when I'm here, too."

"Thanks."

Paul is being short, which means he's thinking.

"You going to get Friday to find out his story?" Friday can pull information from just about anybody.

Just then, the door jingles and Friday walks into the room. "What's wrong?" she asks. She's dressed in her retro gear with bright red lipstick and heels.

"We just hired one of Pete's foundlings to tidy up the place," I tell her.

She presses up onto her tiptoes so she can see him better and whistles. "Oh, he's handsome." Then she notices the wheelchair. "What's his story?"

"We don't know," Paul says. "And you are not to get involved."

She snorts. "Yeah, right." But she's already walking toward Josh.

I know why Pete brought him here. It's because we don't see disabilities. We never have. Living with a brother who's deaf has taught us all to look beneath the surface. The wheelchair this guy is in doesn't bother me at all, although I'd love to know what happened. But not nearly as much as I want to know why he got that tattoo on his cheek.

"I'm going to spank her ass when I get her home," Paul mutters.

"Dude," I say, pretending to gag, "I do not need that much information."

Some military men come in and they're waiting in the lobby area. "I'll take one of them," I say.

Paul nods, and he goes back to stand beside Friday. He puts his hands all over her, almost like he's peeing a virtual circle around her. Finally, she takes his hand and drags him into his office, shutting the door behind them.

Matt goes and bangs on the door. "No getting lucky in the office!" he calls out. He bangs again and again until the door opens and Friday comes out. She's fixing her makeup because Paul has apparently kissed it all off. Paul is wiping his smile as he comes out behind her. "You could have given us a minute," I hear him say to Matt.

"That's just gross, Paul," Matt scolds.

"As gross as it was when you did it with Sky last week?" Paul chuckles. He points to the cameras. "They catch everything, man." He claps Matt on the shoulder.

I want what my brothers have. I'm dying for it. I just wonder if I've found it in Peck. I think so.

I set up my station and start doing tats. It's getting late when I realize that Peck might be at home. At my house. Waiting for me.

I try not to rush my last tat, but it's fucking hard. I still need to run by the store to get ingredients for dinner. But it's all worth it, because I get to see Peck at the end of the day.

Peck

It's late when I get back to Sam's. It's almost midnight, and I'm worried that I'll wake him up. I turn the key and tiptoe into the room. I'm startled when I see that Sam is asleep on the couch. He lifts his head when he hears me moving around.

"Peck?" he asks.

"Yeah," I whisper. I don't know why I'm whispering. It just seems like the thing to do. "Why are you s-still up? It's l-late."

"I was worried about you." He sits up and runs a hand through his hair. Then he presses the heels of his hands into his eyes and rubs.

"I'm s-sorry I w-woke you."

"What took so long?"

I shrug. "It's always a long d-day when we're recording."

He gets up and I see that he's walking. He shuffles over to me and pulls me against his chest, then kisses my forehead. I wrap my arms around his waist, because this feels so right. I take a deep breath as he drags his fingertips up and down my back.

"I thought you weren't coming back," he says.

"I'm sorry. I should I have c-called."

"Have you eaten?" He sets me back a little from him and I miss the heat of him immediately.

"We ordered a pizza around five. Why? Did you cook?"

He takes a plate out of the oven and uncovers it. Now I feel bad. He went to a lot of trouble to cook for me.

He sets the plate on the table and gets me a bottle of water. He holds a chair out. "Sit. I'll keep you company."

"Have you eaten?" I ask him. "We can share."

He props his chin in his hand. "How was recording?"

I groan. "Grueling. We spent hours recording and re-recording." I point to his foot. "You got your walking boot."

He smiles. "Yeah, it's pretty nice not being on crutches."

"How was your meeting this morning?"

He tells me all about what happened, and I'm so glad for him that it wasn't worse.

I look down and see that my plate is almost empty. Crap. I wish I could keep from scarfing down food in front of him, but it's just *so good.*

"You like the chicken?" he asks.

"It was like having sex."

He jerks. "Beg your pardon?"

"Awesome. Breathtaking. Surprising. Comforting." I grin as he shifts in the chair.

"You're comparing my food to sex?"

I nod. "Yep."

"Cupcake, I can guarantee you sex with me will be a lot better than some chicken dinner."

I lay my fork down. I might as well. My plate is empty. "Prove it," I say.

Silence falls over the room like a heavy blanket. "If I thought you were ready for what I want, I would."

He gets up and washes my plate. "How do you know what I'm ready for?" I walk up behind him and pull his shirt from where it's tucked into his pants. I slide my hands around his naked stomach, and lay the side of my face on his shoulder. He goes stiff in my arms.

"I'll give you ten minutes to knock that shit off," he says. He chuckles, and I can feel his belly moving under my fingers. I dip my fingers into his waistband and his hand comes up to cover mine. "You ready to go to bed?" he asks, turning his head to kiss me over his shoulder.

"I need a shower. The sound guy was smoking and I'm afraid I have it in my hair."

He lifts a lock up to his nose and grimaces. "You do."

"Ugh," I grunt.

"Use my bathroom," he says.

The bathroom where he was masturbating to thoughts of me this morning? "Okay."

I grab my things and go into his bathroom. I shower really quickly and brush my teeth.

When I go back into the room, Sam has taken his contacts out and he's wearing glasses in bed, reading a book. "I didn't know you wear glasses," I tell him. I saw him wearing them last night for the first time, but I never would have known otherwise.

"I don't." He takes them off and sets them to the side.

"You do," I tease.

His gaze takes a lingering path up and down my body. I'm wearing a long T-shirt that goes down to my knees and I'm not wearing a bra. His perusal shoots straight to my center.

"I feel bad that you stayed up waiting for me," I tell him. He grabs me and pulls me onto his chest, and I lay my face on the light dusting of hair that graces his body.

"I like waiting for you," he tells me. He lifts his head and kisses my forehead. He reaches over and turns out the light. I can feel him all around me, but I can't see him. "So I was wondering…"

"Ask. Just ask." But I stiffen because I'm not sure I'm going to like whatever he's going to ask me about.

"This thing we're doing. What would you call it?"

I lift my head. "You mean sex?"

He grumbles. "No, *this* is not sex. If you think *this* is sex, your previous partners were really bad at it." He laughs, his chest shaking beneath me. "No, this…relationship." He jostles me in his arms. "This *is* a relationship, right?"

"I guess so," I say quietly.

"You guess?"

"I mean, yeah, I think it's a relationship." I draw a circle on his chest. "Do you want it to be a relationship?" I hold my breath.

"Hell yeah, I want it to be a relationship."

"I wouldn't mind if it was sex, too," I whisper. I kiss the center of his chest, and his belly clenches under my hand.

"Would you be mad if I said I'm not ready for sex yet?" He strokes a hand down the length of my hair.

I scramble away from him, but he wraps me up tightly in his strong arms.

"Don't go," he says. "I don't think you took that the way I meant it."

"How did you mean it?"

"I mean that I really, really like you and I want to see where this thing is going."

"Okay…"

"And I know that once I get to be inside you, I'm never going to want to let you go, so I want to be sure this is permanent."

"Permanent." God, I probably sound like a parrot.

"Permanent."

"So…no sex."

"You okay with that?"

"Well, I was kind of hoping to try out that piercing."

He growls and pulls my earlobe into his mouth to bite it gently. He rolls me onto my back and covers me. His lips touch mine, and his tongue slides into my mouth. When he lifts his head, I've lost all my wits. I can't put two thoughts together.

"You can try out my piercing after you fall in love with me, okay?"

"What?"

"I kind of need for you to love me, Peck." He's quiet but fierce. "You're not in love with me yet, are you?"

"Um…" I don't know how to answer him.

"It's okay. Don't rush it. I can wait."

I can feel his dick pressing against my thigh, and I reach out to touch it. He catches my hand and brings it to his lips. His breath is hot against my fingers, and his lips tickle.

"But this morning—" I protest.

"This morning was me being greedy. I'm sorry about that."

But I came! And he didn't. There's no greed in that. "Huh," I grunt. "I was the only one who got off. I can't figure how you were being greedy."

He chuckles. "You have no idea how long I've wanted to taste you, do you? To smell you and feel you and touch you? To feel you come apart all around my fingers?"

"Jesus," I whisper.

"It's all I thought about all day." He chuckles. "I'm going to have to go and take a cold shower if we keep this up."

"I could…" I reach for him again, but he pulls his hips back.

"No. Not yet." He rolls me so that I'm facing away from him, and pulls me into the spoon of his hips. His dick is pressing hard against my bottom. "He'll give up in a minute. Go to sleep."

His hand slips beneath my shirt and lifts to cup my breast. Thank God! But his hand doesn't keep moving. It stops. I lie there, rigid, waiting for him to make a move. But he goes soft behind me and his breaths fall long and even by my ear, and I realize he's asleep.

He falls asleep cupping my breast, holding me like I'm something precious. I just wish I was.

Sam

She has been here for eleven nights. Eleven nights of holding her while she sleeps. Eleven mornings of waking up with her wrapped around me. Eleven showers where I jack off to thoughts of her, because I'm so fucking horny that I can't even walk. I'm going nuts.

She goes to work every day and so do I. I work out every morning with weights with my trainer, trying to stay in shape so that when it's time to go back to playing, I won't die of exhaustion when I run onto the field. I think the workouts are the only things that keep me from losing my mind. Well, that and masturbation.

She smells so fucking good.

I wrap my arms around her at night, with her bottom nestled in my crotch, and my dick reaching toward her. She wiggles her plump little ass against me and I have to bite the inside of my cheek until I taste copper so that I won't sink inside her. I want to be inside her. More than anything. More than I want to eat. More than I want to cook. More than I want to breathe.

Speaking of breathing…she smells like sunshine and heat. And I get hard again thinking about her.

She's in the shower, and she's been there for a while.

I hear her call to me. Good God, if she calls me in there with her right now, I'll have no choice but to take back my vow to not sleep with her until she falls in love with me.

"Sam," I hear from behind me.

I was pretending to watch a cooking show, but I was really just thinking about her being naked and pretending that my hands were water sliding all over her body. I jam a pillow into my lap.

"Sam," she says again.

"Yeah?"

"I need to get something out of my purse. Can you close your eyes?"

"Why?" I turn to look. She's peeping out from my room, wearing nothing but a towel. I can see the freckled skin of her shoulders, and she has the end of the towel shoved down between her breasts, making plump pillows that billow over the top. God, she's going to kill me. Death by desire? Is that possible? I adjust my junk.

"Sam, I need my phone. Can you close your eyes? Please?" Her voice is quiet. I look at her again and her cheeks are all rosy.

"Are you okay?" I ask.

"Yeah." She waits a beat. "Can you close your eyes?"

"Fine," I bite out.

"Don't look."

"Okay." I heave a sigh. I can hear her naked feet slap against the hardwood floor. Then her footsteps get faster and I imagine she's grabbed her phone and darted back to my bedroom. I look back and see her streak around the corner. The end of the towel barely covers her ass. And what a fine ass it is. It's plump and round and perfect and oh my God those thighs. I want to chase behind her, and I get up to do just that. But she closes my bedroom door with a soft *snick*.

What the fuck?

I press my ear to the door, and I hear her murmuring something. Is she on her phone? I knock lightly on the door. "Are you all right?"

"Yes."

"What are you doing?" I turn the knob, but the door is locked.

"Nothing."

"Are you sure you're all right?"

"Yep."

"Then why is the door locked?"

"Um… Because I wanted to keep you out?" Her voice is soft and it's right by the door.

I test the lock again. "But it's my room." And you're naked inside. Or almost naked. Hell, you're just *in* it. I don't give a fuck what you're wearing. You could have on a suit of armor and I'd still want to be in there with you. That would sound stupid if I said it out loud. So I'm glad I only said it in my head.

"Can you give me a few minutes?" she asks softly. "And let my sisters in when they get here? Please?"

Wait. Her sisters are coming over? "Are you sure you're all right?" I jiggle the door a little harder.

"I'm fine, Sam."

Suddenly, there's a knock on the front door. I walk over and open it, and her four sisters brush past me. Star is carrying a brown paper bag in her hand. "Which way to the boom-boom room?" Wren asks.

I point. Like an idiot. Because I am one.

They all go down the hallway and one of them knocks and says, "The cavalry is here. Duh duh duh duh!" She trumpets the noise like the British are coming.

The door opens and Peck jerks the four of them into the room.

What the fuck just happened?

Peck

I am so stupid. I started my period this afternoon, and I had one tampon left. One. Just one. And then I dropped it. Right into the toilet. Normally, this wouldn't be a problem, because when you have four sisters, there are always feminine hygiene products around. But there are none at Sam's apartment. I don't know if I should be happy about that. I probably should, because if he had some, I'd have to wonder who they belonged to. He didn't. I checked.

So I had no choice but to call my sisters and ask one of them to bring me some. I didn't expect all four of them to show up, but I should have. Nosy bitches.

Star closes the door behind her and then tosses me the paper bag. I disappear into the bathroom, take care of things, and come back out. Now that I can, I pull on panties, and drop a long T-shirt down over my towel, and then tug it free.

"So this is where the magic happens, huh?" Fin asks. She looks around. "Nice digs."

"I kind of expected some kinky shit in here," Wren says. She opens the top drawer of the bedside table. "No dirty magazines or anything," she says.

"Get out of his drawers," I scold, and I walk over and chuck her with my hip. She falls back onto the center of Sam's bed. Then she suddenly sits up.

"Wait!" she cries. "Did you have sex here? On these covers?"

I laugh. "No. No sex. You're safe. Lounge all you want."

I drag a wide-tooth comb through my hair.

"Oh, you poor thing," Fin says. "He's still withholding the goodies?"

"Shut up," I grouse.

"Oh, he *is*." She makes a *tsk-tsk* sound with her teeth. "I'm so sorry for your misfortune."

I decide to be honest. They're my sisters, after all. "I swear to God, if he doesn't make a move soon, I'm going to lose my mind."

Fin points to her crotch. "So, he ate you out that one time, and then he's been hands off ever since?"

"No, not hands off," I admit. "Hands on. All the time. But no sex."

"That's not a bad thing," Star says. Leave it to her to be the voice of reason. "It's good to wait."

"Says Gidget the flying nun," Fin grouses.

"Says the slut of Zero," Star tosses back. She picks up a pillow and throws it at Fin's head. She's laughing, though.

"Don't even try to slut-shame me," Fin says. She pretends to be offended, but we all know she's not.

"Why should she? It wouldn't make a difference." Wren laughs.

Fin has a healthy sexual appetite, and she doesn't sleep with anyone more than once. It's a rule, I think. There's no problem with it, of course—it's her decision what she does with her body—but Star likes to try to reform her every now and then. I don't know why. Fin has no desire or need to change. She's perfectly happy breaking hearts all over New York.

"So why won't he sleep with you?" Lark asks. She picks up a picture of him with all his brothers and their wives. It was taken on a beach. It's really a lovely picture.

"I'm supposed to fall in love with him first," I say quietly.

Fin jumps up. "Fuck that! He wants a fucking commitment? What is this—the stone age?" She laughs out loud.

Star watches my face. "How close are you?"

I toy with a string on the bedspread. "Oh, I'm pretty sure I'm there."

A pillow hits my face. "Shut the fuck up!" Wren cries. "Seriously?"

"You love him?" Star asks quietly.

"I am pretty sure I do."

"How do you know?" Star asks. She's not joking. She looks intently at my face.

"I just…know. I don't know." I flop back on the bed with a groan. "What do I do?"

"Him," Fin calls. "Do him. Then let him do you. Wash. Rinse. Repeat."

"That's not what I meant."

Wren lays her hand on my forehead. "Do you have a fever? No. You're cool as a cucumber."

"I think I love him."

"What's wrong with that?" Star asks.

"We're about to go on tour for six weeks, that's what."

"Will you miss him?"

"Like crazy." My heart hurts at the very thought of it.

"It's just six weeks. If it's real, he'll still be here when you get back."

I nod. "I know."

A knock sounds on the door. "Peck," Sam calls.

I crack the door. "Yes?"

"I'm getting worried," he blurts out.

I open the door wider, so he can see the way my sisters are draped all over his furniture. "Everything is fine."

"Fine, now that we saved the day." Lark raises her arms like she's flexing her muscles. "Zeroes to the rescue."

I point to the door. "Out," I tell my sisters.

Sam leans in the doorway, grinning at them.

"Damn, he's pretty," Wren says as she walks by him.

He grins even more.

"Thank you," I call to their retreating backs.

They all wave at me, and go out the door. But then Fin sticks her head back in. "All your equipment works, right?" she asks Sam. She waves toward his crotch. "I mean that equipment. Not the football equipment."

Sam glances down and grins. "Last time I checked." He scratches his scruffy chin.

"Oh, ok. Just wanted to be sure." She winks at me. "Love you, Peck!" she sings out, and then she closes the door.

Sam chuckles. "So nice that your sisters are worried about my junk."

"Sorry about that."

He narrows his eyes at me. "What was in the bag?"

"Nothing." Heat creeps up my cheeks.

"Was too. What was it?"

"Nothing," I say again. My face is flaming hot. "Are you ready to go to bed?"

He nods, and looks me up and down.

He goes into the bathroom to brush his teeth. He comes back carrying the box of tampons that I thought I'd hidden behind the towels. "You had your sisters bring you tampons?" He laughs. And it's not a snicker. It's a great big belly laugh. I expect him to wipe his eyes any second.

I snatch them out of his hand and stick them back under the counter. "That is not amusing."

"Are you kidding?" he cackles. "That shit's funny as hell." He laughs for a moment and then he finally sobers. "Why didn't you tell me you needed them? I would have gone to the store."

My eyes jerk up. He's serious. "It's kind of a girl thing." I scratch my nose, trying to find something to do with my hands.

"It's a boy thing, too, when a boy's girl needs them. Next time, just tell me and I'll go get them." He kisses my forehead.

"Thanks," I say quietly.

He points to his bedside table. "Why is my drawer open?"

"Oh, ah..." I breathe in. He watches me. "The girls were looking for dirty magazines."

"They're in the bottom drawer," he tosses out casually. Then he goes back into the bathroom and closes the door.

I tiptoe over to the night stand and open the bottom drawer. It makes a racket, and I look over my shoulder to be sure he's not coming out, but I'm nosy and I want to see what he's talking about.

There's nothing in the bottom drawer. I push it shut.

He walks back out of the bathroom.

"Liar," I say.

He laughs and lies back on the bed, resting the back of his head in his hands. "Bottom drawer of the dresser, silly," he tells me. He glares at me in challenge, a spark in his eyes.

I can't help it. I want to see. I open the drawer and then freeze. He wasn't kidding. He has a magazine. And a movie. I pick it up and look at it, and I can feel that blush creep up my face again.

"Want to watch it with me?" he asks innocently. Like he's asking me to watch *Frozen*.

"Um..." Considering that I just got my period, watching the movie might be a lesson in torture. "No thanks. Maybe another time."

"Rain check," he says.

He tosses the covers back and I get in bed with him. He turns off the light and pulls me to lie on his chest.

He takes a breath. "Seriously, Peck," he says. "Next time you need something—anything—just tell me. I'll take care of it."

"Okay," I whisper. After a moment, I say, "This is kind of weird."

"Tampons are not weird. They're necessary. Like shampoo and toothpaste and condoms."

"Yep." I got no response to that.

"Why does it bother you?"

"I don't know." It just seems to be very...*intimate*.

He's quiet. I can feel his chest moving beneath my face. Up. Down. Up. Down.

"Hey Sam, can I tell you something?" I whisper. I lift my face and press my chin into his chest so I can look toward his face in the dark.

"You can tell me anything." He kisses my forehead.

"I think I might be falling in love with you."

His breath stalls.

"Are you okay?" I ask.

"Yeah…"

"Then what's wrong?"

"Nothing." He shifts under me a little, like he's suddenly restless. Then he blurts out, "Are you sure?"

He rolls me over onto my back so he can hover over me. I nod. He groans and presses his face into my neck. "You have no idea how long I've waited to hear that."

"Do you think you might love me too? Someday? Maybe not even now. But someday?" My voice quivers.

"Do you realize that you haven't even stuttered a single time since we've been talking tonight?" he says out of the blue.

I sit up. "What?" Of course I stuttered. I always stutter.

"Not once. Not a single time tonight. That's just about as important to me as your telling me you love me."

"Why?"

"Because it means you're comfortable with me. You trust me. Or at least that's what I tell myself." He waits a second. "Am I wrong?"

He's right. I haven't stammered even once. But suddenly I'm tongue-tied. "I-I don't know what to say."

He pulls me back down to him. "Don't say anything."

He grabs my thigh and pulls my leg across his hips. I nestle into the crook of his shoulder. His hand slides up and down my thigh and then disappears beneath the edge of my panties. "Sam," I warn.

He laughs. "Can't blame a guy for trying."

As I close my eyes, I realize he never really did say he loves me back.

Sam

I go to the tattoo shop early the next day, because I know Paul is on the schedule and I'm hoping he will be alone. I really need to talk to him.

I push through the door and bells jingle over my head. I stop short when I see Josh sitting across the table from Friday. Friday married my oldest brother Paul, and she's almost like a mom to us— that is, if you can count a hot-as-hell pin-up with red lips, short skirts, and high heels as a mom. But she's the closest thing we have.

"Good morning," Friday chirps at me.

I'm really surprised to see her alone here with Josh. Paul can't be far away. He'd never leave her alone for very long with someone he doesn't trust. And this is someone no one should trust. I just have that feeling. He might be in a wheelchair, but he's hard. Too hard.

"Morning," I murmur.

Friday points to Josh. "Josh here was just telling me about where he's from."

"Where's Paul?"

She glares at me. "He's dropping the kids at Matt's house."

I glare back at her. "Why are you here alone?"

"Because someone needed to be here." Her brow furrows and I think she might strangle me if given an opportunity. "Are you working today?"

I shake my head. "No, I just wanted to talk to Paul."

She tilts her head and stares at me. I swear, it makes me twitchy when she does that shit. "Everything okay?" she asks.

"Fine."

I sit down in a rolling chair and start to spin in it.

Josh rolls toward the back of the shop and disappears into the supply room.

"You could be a little more welcoming!" she hisses at me.

"Why the fuck are you here alone with him, Friday?" I hiss back. "You know he could be dangerous."

She shakes her head. "He's not."

"Fuck," I breathe. "How do you know that?" I glare at her. "You don't."

"I do." She lifts her nose in the air. "I just have a feeling."

"When will Paul be here?" I ask. No fucking way I'm leaving until he gets here, particularly now that I know she's here alone with the ex-con.

She nods toward the back of the shop, toward Josh-the-ex-con-who-she-thinks-is-a-teddy-bear, and says, "We're filming today. The cameras are going to love him."

I stop spinning. "Does he know he's going to be filmed?"

She nods. "That's what we were just talking about."

"And he's okay with that?"

She nods. "Apparently. He stayed, didn't he?" She does that head-tilty thing again and just looks at me. "So, what did you want to talk to Paul about?"

Friday was in the room the last time Paul gave me advice about Peck, so she knows all about my fears. "Just guy talk," I tell her anyway, because she's being nosy.

"Sex talk," she clarifies. "You need some condoms? There's a whole drawer full at home."

Suddenly the door opens and Pete rushes in. He's all smiles and he reaches into his back pocket and pulls out a cigar made of bubble gum. "We're pregnant!" he yells.

Friday grins and runs to him. He catches her against him and he swings her around. "So happy for you two," she says and she kisses Pete's cheek. "Is Reagan with you?" She looks over his shoulder.

"Nah, she's at home puking her guts out." He laughs. "Nasty stuff, that morning sickness."

"And you left her alone while she's sick?" Friday slugs him on the arm.

"Actually, she threw me out." He starts to mock her voice. "If you don't get the fuck out of my face, I'm going to drop-kick you into the middle of next week." He laughs. "She probably even meant it.

Usually when she's pissed at me, she threatens my balls. So I'm pretty sure she didn't want me around watching her heave. Plus, I wanted to come and check on Josh. Is he here?"

Friday points toward the rear of the shop and Pete goes in that direction.

"I can't believe he was allowed to breed," I say quietly.

"He's going to make a wonderful father." She makes a happy little inhale. Then she narrows her eyes. "So, how's Peck?"

"She's fine."

"And?" She does that cute little brow arch and her eyebrow piercing goes sideways.

"And nothing." I cross my arms in front of my chest and pretend to pout.

"And everything." She picks up a piece of paper from the table next to her, balls it up, and throws it at my head.

I deflect it with my arm. "What was that for?"

"For lying."

"I'm not lying," I protest.

"Then let's try again. How's Peck?"

"She's still fine, just like she was thirty seconds ago."

"Why are you here, Sam?" She taps the heel of those ridiculously high heels.

I throw up my hands. "Can't a guy just come by to chat?"

The bells over the door jingle again and I turn to look. Thank God it's Paul.

"Did you know your wife was here alone with the new guy?"

Paul stares at her for a second, then he marches forward, grabs her elbow and pulls her into the office.

Oh, crap. She's going to kill me for ratting her out.

They come out a few minutes later, and she won't even look in my direction. She goes to the back and disappears.

"She's going to kill me," I mutter.

"Don't fall asleep around her any time soon," he warns. "She knew not to be alone with him. I'd already told her, but she's too fucking nosy for her own good." He looks at me. "How's the leg?"

"Better."

"And Peck?"

"Peck's leg is fine."

"Dickwad," he mutters. He looks up and I suddenly have all his attention. "Is everything all right?"

"Yeah." I heave a sigh and drop my face into my hands.

"Then what's up?"

"She told me she loves me," I blurt out.

His eyes open wide. "Wow."

Wow? That's all I get?

He starts setting up his machines. "How do you feel about that?"

"I fucking love it." My heart thrills.

"But?"

"But I'm just not sure."

He laughs. "No one ever is. You just have to go with your gut. If it's meant to be, you'll meet her somewhere near the middle and fall in love with her too."

"Oh, I already did."

He looks up and smiles. "Really?"

A grin tips the corners of my lips. "Yeah."

"What does love mean to you?" he asks.

"It means that if something happened to her tomorrow, I don't know if I would ever be the same."

"Love does that to you."

"Did you feel like Friday was yours long before *she* knew she was yours?"

He laughs. "I knew she was mine the first time I kissed her. Then I just had to convince *her*."

"Do you ever feel like you dragged her along? Like maybe it wasn't her idea?"

He shakes his head. "Never. Is that what you feel like you're doing with Peck?"

I run a hand through my hair. "I don't know. She told me she loves me. And she sleeps in my bed every night. And now if she left me, she'd leave a hole behind. That's all."

"Has she talked to her mom yet?"

I shake my head. "Not that I know of. That's kind of why she's with me. So she can stay away from her mom."

"Maybe she needs to face that. Then she could at least be with you by choice rather than by necessity. You'd probably feel a little bit more comfortable about her reason for being there if you knew she was there for you, and not just for the safety of your apartment." He shrugs. "But what do I know. I had to have Friday lead me around by my dick piercing to get it." He grins.

"So, do you think she might?" I ask quietly.

"I think she's an idiot if she doesn't."

"She's going on tour soon."

"How do you feel about that?"

"I'm going to miss her like crazy."

"Be sure to tell her that."

"I will."

"You know Logan and Emily are going to be traveling with them, right?" He gets a gleam in his eye.

"Yeah. Why?"

"Just saying."

I just wish I knew *what* he was just saying.

"So, you're the last one to fall," he says. He's serious all of a sudden. "I never really worried about you. I worried more about Pete, because I knew *you* had more ability to love than any of the rest of us."

"What makes you say that?"

"I don't know," he hedges. "You just wore your heart on your sleeve. You love, and you love well and true. That's one of your strengths."

"I'm not sure if *strength* is the right word."

"A lot of men would be put off by her stutter. Embarrassed by it. You're not, are you?"

"I don't even notice it when she does it, but last night we had a whole conversation without her stuttering even once."

"She's learning to trust you."

"God, I hope so."

"She reminds me a lot of Emily with her dyslexia. She fought so hard to hide it until she met Logan, and then she pretty much had to learn to trust him, and know that he saw all of her and not just her disability. Is that what Peck's doing?"

"I don't know what you mean."

"It sounds like she's learning to trust you. She told you she loves you. She talks. She talks without stuttering. It sounds like you've assured her that it's the whole package you're in love with. Not just parts of her."

"She grew up in foster care."

He nods. "I know. She told Friday about it. It was pretty hard for her until Emilio took one look at her and found a daughter."

That warms my heart. "Is that how it happened? I thought they just went for ice cream and he took her home, along with all the others."

"Ask her. Hell, ask him."

I nod. I will. "So, when do I tell her I love her? Without scaring her?"

"You didn't tell her when she told you?"

"I couldn't...hell, I couldn't talk."

He laughs. "God, that's a good feeling, isn't it?"

"Not particularly."

"No, it's perfect," he corrects me. "Your heart is in your throat and your head starts to swim and you suddenly can't talk, all because your heart is too full. That's when you know she's the right one. It's when the emotions slap you in the face and you don't care."

"Do you think I'll ever play football again? I mean, the way I used to?"

"I think you can do anything you want to do. I didn't raise any quitters."

"What if I don't want to play ball for the rest of my life?"

He shrugs. "Do what you want to do."

"When I first started, I wanted it because there was more money involved than I could ever imagine having."

"What did you want the money for?"

"To take care of my family. Pete went to jail trying to take care of everyone. And I should have too."

"But you didn't. You got an opportunity most people only dream of."

"Exactly."

"With that said, though, you need to set yourself up with things you love. Not things you can only tolerate. A woman you love. An occupation you love. A home you love. Children you love. If you settle, you'll never be happy. Not really."

I spin my chair around. "You love what you do, right?"

"Always have."

"Good."

"What are you going to do?"

"Finish out my contract and see how it goes."

"I meant about Peck, doofus."

I laugh. "Oh, I guess I'm going to tell her how I feel, and grab her and stick her in a closet when she runs screaming in the other direction."

"Something tells me you're worried for nothing."

I hedge. "I don't know."

"You're smart, dedicated, sympathetic, and you have the ability to love her unlike anyone ever has. Stop doubting yourself."

"Yes, sir."

Stop doubting myself. I'll get right on that.

Peck

Emily is in the sound booth working on her new single, recording the lyrics. The background we laid down two weeks ago will be added later.

She has the purest voice I have ever heard. It resonates with the listener, reverberates around in your head, and comes out all your pleasure centers. The hair on my arms stands up, and I look down at Kit, Emily and Logan's daughter, and she pats my cheek. I'm standing outside the booth holding her while her mom works. I take her hand in mine, press it to my mouth, and blow a razzberry onto her tender skin. She squeals and giggles, and then pats my face again. "'G'in," she says.

I blow into her palm and she laughs. Kit is walking and starting to talk.

What did she say? Logan asks me in sign language.

Again, I tell him. *She wanted me to blow on her hand again.*

She reaches for her daddy and he takes her from me, hoisting her into his arms. She bounces in his arms and he laughs.

"I want to hear her talk," he says out loud.

What? I ask him. What could he possibly mean by that?

Em and I went to talk to a doctor last week. I'm scheduled for surgery right before we leave on the tour. He looks at me. *Going to get a cochlear implant. Then they'll activate it when the tour is over.*

Seriously? I never imagined he would do that.

He nods. *I don't want to miss anything. I already missed her first word. I can't hear her cry in the night. I can't tell if she's calling for me. I can't hear her laugh.* He looks toward Emily in the booth, where's she's perched on a stool with a guitar in her lap. She smiles at him and kisses her palm, then blows it toward him. He grins, reaches for the flying imaginary kiss, and tucks it into his pocket. He turns back to me. Kit has laid her head on his chest, and she snuggles under his chin. He lazily strokes her back, and her eyes start to drift closed. He talks with his hands behind her back. *I can feel when she needs me, but I can't hear it.* He shakes his head.

Deafness is a culture—a strong one. This much I know. For him to get an implant, he must feel very strongly about his desire to hear, to experience all the sounds he'll miss with having a daughter.

That can't be an easy decision for you.

It's not. I haven't even told my brothers yet.

Seriously? He told me and he hasn't told them?

Em's the only one who knows. I'm still working it out in my head.

Are you ready for the tour?

I'm ready to see her get to play her music for everyone. He nods toward her. *She's made for this stuff.*

I'm glad you're going with her.

She's my heart. I'd stop breathing if I couldn't be with her.

He says it like he's saying he wants a pastrami sandwich. Like his words don't pack an emotional punch. Like what he's saying isn't pivotal.

She's the air I breathe. She's the food that keeps me from starving. She's the mother of my child. He shakes his head. *A couple of years ago, I never would have thought this feeling could be possible.*

What feeling?

The feeling that she is the only thing I need to survive. I used to fuck women. That's all. Then I met her. He looks at her through the glass. *And I didn't fuck her, because I couldn't bear to lose her.*

I don't even know how to respond to that.

How are things going with Sam?

Fine.

Fine? He grins.

Heat creeps up my cheeks. *Fine.* I want to ask him so many questions about Sam.

He's pretty taken with you.

Taken? What does that even mean?

Absorbed. Entranced by. He really, really likes you.

How do you know?

He snorts. *Because you got him all tongue-tied all the time. He doesn't know up from down. Left from right. Top from bottom. That boy is taken.* He lifts a hand and chucks my shoulder. But then he gets really serious. *Honestly, I've never seen him with anyone the way he is with you.*

What do you mean?

He avoids my eyes. *He used to be a little bit of a horn dog. But he dropped all that the moment he met you. He's different. It's like you fill him with possibility.*

I lay a hand on my chest. *That's not me. That's just him. He is one big possibility, all by himself.*

You see him as more than he is. That's why you're good for him.

He's a professional football player. Seriously? He's the shit. He knows he's the shit.

He's a man. And he has the same insecurities as the rest of us. His hands stop moving for a minute. They're almost hesitant when they start back up. *It hasn't been easy for us. We had a mom who was awesome. And a dad who wasn't. But even with all we were lacking, we had each other. That was never in doubt.*

So, where's the problem?

The problem is that we had no example of love. We had no idea what to look for. Then we found it and BAM! He smacks his palm against his forehead. *Hits you like a ton of bricks.*

No ton of bricks has hit Sam yet. I told him I love him and he didn't reciprocate.

Logan winces before he speaks, and I brace myself for what's coming.

If you don't feel the same way he does, just tell him. Don't lead him on. And don't hurt him. He's more invested than you think.

Emily pushes the mic back and gets up from her stool. He opens the door to go in to her, closing it softly behind him, leaving me completely alone with my thoughts. But they're scattered into such disarray that I don't know how to put them together.

Part of the reason that I'm here instead of at Sam's apartment is that I needed some space to think. I needed to find out where my head is, and it's not here in this room. It's with Sam.

Once, I thought life was all about the music. It filled my soul, opened my mouth, and allowed my sound to come out. It gave me a voice. But now…now I'm not so sure that life is about music. I think it might be about more than that, but I don't know what that *more* is.

I let myself out of the studio. My sisters went home a while ago, and I just stayed because I didn't want to go home yet. Logan and Emily are in the sound booth so Emily can hear the sound track. Her voice wafts over the speakers, and Logan is oblivious to it. It's like a gift for the ears—for the soul. But he can't hear it.

They're so different, but they make it work. Hearing Logan talk about his feelings for Emily, it gives me hope. It makes me think there is more to this life than what I've been given. More than what I've taken for myself.

***

I get out of the cab at Sam's apartment. I have worried over it the whole way here. I need to have a talk with Sam and I don't even know where to start. I need to know how he feels about me. I love him, and I told him so. I thought it was what he wanted to hear.

I'm so wrapped up in my own thoughts that I don't even see her. But I hear her say my name. Or at least I hear her say the name I used to have.

"Renee!" she calls.

I spin around and look at the bench beside the apartment building. My mother is sitting there with her knees pulled up to her chest, her skinny arms wrapped around them. Her hair is long and dark like mine, but hers is stringy and greasy.

"What do you want?" I ask.

She stubs out her cigarette, her hand shaking all the while. "I just wanted to talk to you. You're too good for your mama, now?" she asks.

"My *mama* is Marta Vasquez. She's the woman who took me in when you gave me away. She raised me. I'll never be too good for her.

You on the other hand…" I let my voice trail off as I drag my eyes up and down her body.

She gets to her feet. "I see. That's how it is, huh?"

"What do you want? Just say it." I heave out a sigh. Maybe once she makes her demands, she'll go away.

"I need some help."

"Of course you do," I murmur. "You always did."

Her eyes narrow as she gazes at my face. "You finally outgrew that awful stutter."

No, I didn't. I've been beating a rhythm with my thumb on my pant leg ever since I started talking to her. "There's nothing wrong with my stutter. There never was."

She scoffs. "You couldn't put two words together."

"I don't remember you ever wanting to hear two words I had to say."

She rolls her bloodshot eyes. "I'm in a little bit of trouble," she suddenly blurts out.

"What kind of trouble?"

"The kind where there are people after me."

"What did you do?"

"I took something that didn't belong to me. And I owe some people some money for it."

Usually, that means she stole something and hocked it to buy drugs, or she just stole money from someone. "How much?"

"Ten thousand," she says quietly.

"That's all?"

Her eyes fly wide open. *"That's all?"* She sneers. "Sometimes I forget that you're a superstar now. You're probably wiping your ass with hundred dollar bills."

Suddenly, the door of the apartment building opens and Sam walks out. He comes straight to me. "You okay?" he asks, taking my elbows in his hands. He looks into my eyes.

I shrug him off, because I really don't want to be touched right now. Just being near my mother makes me feel dirty, and I don't like it. "I'm fine."

He nods and then turns to my birth mother. "Sam Reed," he says, and he sticks out his hand like she's someone he should want to impress. I want to jerk his hand back because I'm afraid he'll catch something. "Nice to meet you," he says as he shakes her hand. I'm actually surprised she touched him.

"Who are you?" she asks.

"I'm Peck's boyfriend."

She looks at me. "Peck? What kind of a fucked-up name is that?" She glares at Sam. "Her name is Renee."

Peck is the name that two loving parents gave to me when I desperately needed a new start. Tears burn the backs of my eyelids and I blink hard to push them back. "My name is Peck," I say, correcting her.

She glowers at me, but she doesn't argue.

"She wants ten thousand dollars," I tell Sam.

"For what?" he asks.

"None of your fucking business," she snarls.

Sam thrusts me behind him. "It is my fucking business," he says as he points a finger at her. "I am in love with her, and I'm pretty sure she feels the same way about me. So everything about her is my fucking business."

My heart starts to pound. He said it. He finally said it. I take his hand in mine and squeeze it. He looks down at me and brushes a lock of hair behind my ear.

He turns back to her. "I'll ask you again. What do you want the money for?"

A short pause. "Bone." Not more than that. Just one word.

Sam freezes. "Bone."

She nods. "I owe him some money and I need to pay him back."

"Why should she help you?"

"Because if she doesn't, he's going to kill me." Fear skitters across her face, and I know that she believes it.

"Why is this our problem?" Sam crosses his arms in front of his chest. He said *our* problem. Ours. Not mine. My gut clenches.

"I don't have anyone else to go to."

"We'll think about it." He rocks his head toward Henry, who is standing in the doorway with a baseball bat in his hand. He slaps it against his palm over and over. Henry is older, but I like that he's on my team. My team rocks. "Leave your contact information with Henry. We'll call you if we decide to help."

He tugs my hand very gently and pulls me toward the elevator.

"You can't just leave me hanging," she protests.

I can't stand it anymore. I just can't. I rush toward her and stick my finger in her face. She freezes, maybe because of something she sees in my eyes? I don't know. "You left *me* h-hanging for years. You left me alone for d-days. Months. Years. Where were y-you? You left me w-waiting. I used to sit up at night and wait for you to come home, until finally I just stopped waiting. I stopped hoping. So you don't fucking get to fucking tell me you're tired of waiting, bitch."

"Okay," she says quietly.

I fucking hate that I just stuttered in front of her. Sam tugs my hand and I walk with him to the elevator. I suddenly feel like the weight of the world is on my shoulders.

I don't let a single tear fall over my lashes until the elevator doors close.

"Come here, cupcake," I hear Sam say softly. He pulls me against him and holds me close as I sob on his shoulder.

I pull myself together when the elevator stops on our floor. Sam leads me into the apartment and over to the sofa. He sits down and tugs me onto his lap. I curl into him and he holds me close.

"It's been so long since I've seen her," I say when the hiccupping sobs finally subside.

"I know." He rubs my back.

"She still looks the same. But it's wrong. So wrong."

"I know."

"She didn't even come to see me. She just came for money."

"Yes, she did."

"She doesn't care. She never did." My voice breaks again, and I want to kick myself for letting her get to me like this.

"I know."

"What should I do?"

"What do you want to do?"

"I want her to go away! I want her to have never existed. Ever. I want a do-over."

He hums, but doesn't say anything.

"But if I had a do-over, I wouldn't have Emilio and Marta, or any of my sisters. And without them, I wouldn't have you." I look up. "I do have you, right?"

"You got me, cupcake."

"I'm squishing you." I move to get up, but he holds me tightly.

"I'm made of stronger stuff than you might think."

"You told her you love me," I say quietly.

He goes still under me. His hand stops sweeping down my hair. "Do you?"

He turns my head with a finger under my chin so he can look into my eyes. "You doubt it?"

"Well," I hedge, "I told you yesterday and you didn't tell me back, so I didn't know."

"Oh, fuck," he breathes. "I thought it was a given."

"A given?"

"God, I can't breathe when I'm around you, Peck. I can't think. I love you, and I don't want to be apart from you. Ever."

"You love me." It's not a question this time.

The birds in my head start to sing, and my heart does this happy *glug-glug* thing in my chest.

"Yes, I fucking *love you*."

I press my lips to his. He kisses me, softly and tenderly, until I press harder, and our teeth clack together. Then he's right there with me. His tongue slides into my mouth, and its velvety rasp tickles alongside mine. He pushes me back a little and looks into my face, then brushes my hair back with gentle fingers. "Tell me what you want."

"You," I say. "Just you."

"You got me," he whispers against my lips.

I feel like there was dry tinder in my heart, just waiting for a flame. And suddenly, I've been ignited.

"It's late," he says. "Do you want to go to bed?"

I nod. "Yes, please."

I can feel his smile against my cheek. "Okay."

He lifts me off of him and I get to my feet. My legs are a little wobbly and I suddenly am so tired.

We walk into the bedroom and I get in the shower really quickly. Then I get out, wrap myself in a towel, and go into the bedroom so I can put on something to sleep in. Then I move toward the bathroom sink so I can brush my teeth. Sam follows me. He stops behind me and looks at my face in the mirror. "You're so beautiful," he says, as he sets his hands on my hips and his chin on my shoulder.

My mouth is full of toothpaste, so I can't answer.

"I want to fuck you so bad," he says.

I choke on toothpaste.

Sam

She's so fucking beautiful that I can't breathe. My dick is hard and I want to bend her over the counter and slide inside her wet heat. But I know I can't.

I kiss the side of her neck and she tilts her head to give me more. Her eyes close and her head falls back onto my shoulder.

My fingers are shaking a little as I slide them around her waist and dip into the waistband of her panties. Her eyes fly open and she lays her hand over mine to stop me.

"You're still on your period, right?" I ask quietly.

She nods, her cheeks suddenly flaming. "You want to do it in the shower?" she asks. She laughs, but it's not a joyful sound.

Her voice is hesitant, but she meets my eyes in the mirror. I chuckle. "When I finally get to fuck you, it's going to take a while. It certainly won't be a quickie in the shower."

"But—"

"I can wait."

"I can't," she complains.

I laugh. "Don't worry. I'll take care of you."

Her breath hitches. But she doesn't tell me no, not even when I slide my fingers across the hip of her panties, tracing the line all the way around to her back.

I grasp her thick thighs and slide my hands up, rubbing all that delicious flesh that I have been dying to see plump around my fingers.

Her panties are blue, and the hip is nothing more than a tiny string of fabric. "God, these are sexy." I bend down and kiss her hip, lifting her shirt a little.

I inch my way up her back with my lips, taking time to taste her. By the time I get to the center of her back, she's squirming in my arms.

I know she's self-conscious, so I don't take all her clothes off. I lift her shirt, though, and push it up so that I can see her tits.

"Oh, my God," I breathe close to her ear. She shivers in my hold and raises one arm so that her hand can clasp the back of my neck.

Her tits fill my hands and then some. They're big and round, with dark, ruddy nipples. I lift them gently, because I don't know yet how she likes for them to be touched. She covers one of my hands with hers and squeezes.

"Harder?" I ask.

She nods. I can barely feel it, but I see the acceptance in her eyes.

I grasp her nipples between my thumbs and forefingers, each hand full of her, and give them a gentle squeeze. I watch her face in the mirror, and I see that she's watching me just as closely. I wonder if she can see that I'm about to come in my pants. I wonder if she has any idea at all of how she can undo me.

She whimpers and I let her breast drop with my left hand, and I slide it down the tender skin of her belly. Her stomach is a soft, padded lump, and I spread my hand across it. I can almost imagine my child growing there.

"Sam…"

"What?" I whisper back.

I suck her earlobe into my mouth and nip it, while I tug on her nipple, elongating it with gentle pulls. The skin of her neck is a dusky pink, and her mouth hangs open.

"Sam," she says again.

"I like seeing you naked," I tell her. I almost expect her to kick me, but she doesn't. She closes her eyes for a second, and then takes a breath and opens them back up. She looks into my face as I slide my fingers into the waistband of her panties and dip down into her heat. "I know you're on your period. I promise not to touch anything you don't want me to."

She nods. I wonder if she's past the point of caring. Then her hand covers mine and applies pressure, and I know she is. She's past the point where she cares what I see or what I touch.

I dip into her heat and accidentally brush the string of her tampon. I move my fingers by it and circle her clit.

I fucking love that she's letting me be this intimate with her. I fucking love that she's letting me see her. All of her.

She cries out when I swirl my finger around her clit, and I brush up closer to her. My dick presses hard against her bottom. "Take your dick out," she says.

I freeze with my hand in her panties. "I'm a little busy here." No way in hell I'm going to take my hand out of her panties. Not unless she seriously wants me to.

She reaches behind her and grabs the waist of my gym shorts, and then shoves them down until my dick is free. The little fucker heads right for the crack of her ass. Her panties are covering her, though, so I rock against her. My balls are trying to crawl up my throat, and I don't know how much longer I can go on like this. It's too good. And I haven't even been inside her.

God, I want to be inside her.

She reaches behind her and pulls the rear of her panties down. Her ass cheeks are exposed, and they're so round and so perfect that I can't take my eyes off them. She has these beautiful little dimples that only come with a perfect, wide ass. With a gentle hand at the center of her back, I push her forward. I keep my hand on her clit, rubbing in small circles, and she pushes her bottom back against me. But with my free hand, I plump her ass with my palm. I have to close my eyes to keep from coming.

"I'm so close!" she cries. "Sam, please don't make me come alone."

"Oh, fuck yeah," I groan. I spit into my palm and rub it along my dick, getting it wet to ease the friction I'm about to create. Because no way I'm not going to touch her. "I need you," I grit out.

"I can take the tampon out," she says. But she's looking a little flustered. I can see her clearly in the mirror with her shirt rucked up around her throat. Her panties are down around her thighs.

I replace my fingers with hers. "Rub your pussy for me."

I sink my dick in the crack of her ass and slide forward. It's not tight enough, so I palm her cheeks and push them around my dick. She's slick and wet from my spit, and I know this isn't optimal, but I can't seem to stop myself. I don't want to fuck her ass. I just want to press her cheeks closed around my dick. I want to hold all that perfect, plump flesh.

Her fingers slide, circling her clit. I can feel the glancing blow of them every few sweeps as she falters and bumps my balls. "Holy Christ," I swear.

I have her ass in my hands, and I am afraid I'm not going to be able to wait for one more minute. Then she cries out.

Oh, holy hell, she's coming. She's coming hard. Her body quakes and shivers and all I can do is hold onto her ass and thrust through the crease of it. It's not as good as getting to be inside her, but it's close. She's still riding the wave when my balls finally win. I spill myself in the center of her back, shoving through the wet crease of her ass over and over until I'm spent.

She goes still beneath me, putting all of her weight onto the bathroom counter. She smiles softly. She looks so fucking hot like this, with her naked ass in the air, and those soft lips turned up in a satisfied smile.

"That was intense," I say. "Be still and I'll clean you up."

"Shower with me," she says.

I turn on the water and wait a moment, while I help her get up. Her legs are like noodles and she's having trouble even standing. She yawns.

I yank her shirt over her head, pull her into the shower with me, wash her quickly, and then I wash myself.

When we're clean, I wrap her in a clean towel and leave her in the bathroom just in case she needs to take care of girly things. She comes out a minute later and pulls the towel off. She puts on a pair of panties and nothing else. She's not even bashful about it. She slides between my covers almost naked and I fucking love it. I turn off the light and she curls up on my chest. Her fingertips draw a figure eight from one nipple to the other.

"Why did you do that?" she suddenly asks.

"Do what?"

"Most men wouldn't settle for just that."

I scoff. "I'll settle for anything you'll give me. If you just want to hold my hand, I'll settle for that too." I chuckle. "Give me whatever, cupcake. I'll take it."

"That was intense."

I cup my hands in the air, even though I know she can't see me. "Your ass, oh my God…"

She sits up a little. "What about it?"

I laugh. "I fucking *love* it."

She settles back against me. "You don't think there's too much of it?"

I chuckle. "That's like too much Santa Claus. Or too much World Series. Too much Super Bowl. Never happen." I kiss her forehead. "You got a perfect ass, you know?"

She laughs. "I think you're fuck-drunk."

More like love-drunk. "What do you want to do about your mother?"

She goes still in my arms, and I'm suddenly terrified.

"I guess that since she knows I'm here, I should leave."

My heart is suddenly in my throat, and I have to swallow past it. "I can protect you if you stay here."

"Why did you come downstairs when you did?"

I'm guessing she means tonight. "Henry called me. He keeps an eye on you."

"I like Henry." She snuggles into my shoulder.

"He's the best." I run my fingers up and down her naked back. "Why didn't you have a driver? Or security?"

She shrugs. "It was late. I was hanging with Logan and Emily and we got to talking. I didn't realize how late it was." She lifts her face so that her chin sticks in my chest. Her mouth is close to mine. "Watching them together made me miss you. Lots."

"Who? Logan and Em?"

Her voice goes quiet. "And their baby."

Does she want a baby? Does she want a family? With me? My heart fills with hope.

"She's such a good mother."

"She would disagree with you on that. She's still learning."

"All it takes is a mom who actually cares. I wouldn't know what that's like."

"Do you want kids?"

I remember the last time we had this talk. She wasn't sure, because she didn't want her speech disability to impair a child.

"Yeah. I want at least one. And I want to adopt. I want to find a kid like me, one with no hope and no prospects. Maybe even one with a disability. I want to change a kid's life." She wiggles in my arms. "What about you?"

"I want whatever you want."

She freezes. "But what do *you* want?"

"I want you. The rest is negotiable. I'd like to start with one kid. Ours. Adopted. I don't care. I want to have a family that's as close as I am with my brothers."

"You'd be okay with adopting?"

"Have you seen Matt's family at all? His oldest three kids were adopted, and they are family. They're loved just as much as his biological kids."

"That sounds nice." She rolls in my arms so that she's facing away from me. I brush her hair down between us, and kiss her naked shoulder. "I love you, Sam," she whispers.

I can barely hear her, but I do. The words roll around in my mind and in my heart, swelling and growing from a tiny seed into something bigger. "I love you too."

My gut clenches, because I'm afraid she's going to hate me. Something has to be done about her mother. And I'm the man who is going to do it.

***

Paul slams his palm down onto the table. "Abso-fucking-lutely not!" he bellows. He jumps to his feet. "Have you lost your motherfucking mind?"

I called this meeting with my brothers because I need a plan. Logan's the only one who's not here, and I have no idea where he is.

"I don't have a choice," I tell Paul quietly. "I have to go and see him. Peck's mom might not have been around for a while, but she's Peck's birth mother. I need to take care of this for her."

Pete watches me closely. He spent two years behind bars because of Bone. I know he's going to have a problem with this. But he doesn't say anything. Not yet.

"*No*," Paul bites out.

"You don't get a say in this, Paul. I'm asking for your help. Not for permission."

He stops his pacing and stares at me. "What does Peck say about this?"

"She doesn't know."

Paul points a finger at me. "Tell her and then get back to us. Once she dumps your stupid ass. And it'll be all your fault."

Pete glares at me from his seat on the other side of the table. "You know what Bone did to me."

"I know that you and I got caught doing stupid shit and that he was in the middle of it, but we chose to do it."

I'll never forgive myself for the fact that Pete spent two years in jail while I was in college enjoying myself, learning, growing, and being a young man with prospects. Pete's a felon and I'm not, but I should be. Regardless, we chose to commit the crime. Bone paid us for it, but we chose it.

"I'm not going to go and work for him. I'm just going to go and give him the money for Peck's mom. That's all."

"Why can't you just give the money to her mom? Then she can pass it on and everyone can be done with it." Leave it to Pete to be Mr. Sunshine.

"Because I want to be sure it's all the way over. Done. Complete. Bone isn't going to do anything to me. He has no beef with me whatsoever."

Suddenly, a voice from the back of the shop calls out, "I'll go with you."

I look up and see Josh rolling toward us.

"I know Bone," he says. He uncovers his shoulder and shows us a tattoo on the side of his neck.

"Fuck," Paul says. "I fucking knew it." He drops his head into his hands and scrubs his face. He lifts his head, looks at Pete and says, "Show him the door."

"Hear him out," Pete says.

"I know where he works. I know where he lives. I can take you there and be sure you come out safe."

Paul swears. "You can't guarantee he'll be safe."

"I can't guarantee it, no, but I can help. Without me, you'll never get through the front door."

That teardrop tattoo on his cheek freaks me the fuck out.

"When can you go?" I ask.

He shrugs. "I need a couple of days to make a plan."

"A plan for what?" Paul barks.

"I need to find out where he is and what he's doing. I need to be sure he'll be receptive to visitors. The nature of his business is rolling. I'll ask some questions and find out."

I nod. "Okay."

Paul jumps up so fast that his chair flips over. He storms toward the back of the shop.

Matt reaches over and taps the table in front of me. "Let me know when you're going to meet him."

No way in hell I'm taking any of my brothers with me. They have families. Kids. Wives.

I have Peck. And I'm doing this for her, I remind myself.

"I need to see him anyway," Josh says. "I need to give him something."

"Bone?" I ask.

He nods. Then he rolls toward the back of the shop and picks up a plunger. He wheels himself into the bathroom and the door closes behind him.

"Do you need any money?" Matt asks.

"I'm good." I have more money than I could dream of. And nothing to spend it on.

"I hope this all works out like you hope." Matt squeezes my hand again and then he goes to his station and starts to set up for the day.

My only hope is that I'm doing the right thing.

Peck

A knock sounds on the door and I go look through the peephole. Emily and Logan are kissing on the other side of the door, with Kit smushed between them.

"God, you two are like r-rabbits," I say as I open the door.

Emily buries her face in Logan's chest. After a second, she raises her pink cheeks and looks at me. I step back and she walks into the apartment with Logan and Kit following her.

"Thanks for doing this," she says as she drops a diaper bag onto the sofa and starts to unpack it. "These are her favorite toys. And her food is in here. She's not picky, and she knows signs for her favorite things, so don't be surprised if you see her use them."

I'm happy to babysit Kit. I'm just really surprised they asked me. They usually use a network of the brothers and their wives. "Do you two have big p-plans today?"

Logan points to his ear. "Pre-op appointment."

"Do your b-brothers know?" Surely Sam would have mentioned it to me.

He shakes his head. "We wanted to do this alone. So I'd appreciate it if you could keep it to yourself."

"You want me to l-lie to him?"

"No…" He shakes his head. "We're putting you in a bad spot, aren't we?"

"You really should t-tell them." Their feelings are going to be hurt if he does this without them. "It's a big deal and you need your family for this."

Emily punches his shoulder. "See, I told you so. You need to tell them."

He swipes a hand down his face. "Okay. After this appointment, I'll tell them that I'm giving up my culture so that I can have an operation. That I'm taking back all the ways they changed for me so that I can hear. It was all for nothing. Their learning to sign. Their learning to communicate with me. Their lifestyle changes, like flashing phone monitors, and captioned television all the time. It was all for nothing."

"You're not nothing," Emily tells him. "And that's exactly why they learned everything they did. And you're not changing. You're not giving up anything."

I feel like I shouldn't be here, so I bend down and pick Kit up. She lets me lift her in my arms and she starts to babble at me.

"What did she say?" Logan asks. I can hear his teeth grinding as he waits for my response.

"Nothing, really," I tell him.

"See, that's what I need to know."

"I get it," I tell him. And I totally do.

"What we don't get is why you feel the need to do this alone." Emily isn't pulling any punches with him at all.

He wraps his arm around Emily's shoulder and pulls her against him. "I'm not alone."

Emily rolls her eyes and hands me a piece of paper with phone numbers on it. "Call me if anything goes wrong, okay? We should be gone at least until this afternoon." She hugs me really quickly. "And thank you for doing this. I didn't know who else to ask. I mean, I could have asked one of the others, but then I'd have to lie about where we're going and I didn't want to do that." She glares at Logan. "I still don't want to do that."

"One of the others?" I'm not sure what she meant by that.

"One of the other Reed girls." She grins at me. "You're officially a Reed Significant Other." She starts to tick items off on her fingers. "So, you're officially invited to girls' night, makeover parties, and shopping trips." She jerks a thumb toward Kit. "And babysitting." She grins.

Honestly, I feel honored she even asked me to watch Kit.

Emily hands me a toy. "If you'll shake this around and make lots of noise, we'll sneak out the door when she's not looking."

I take the toy and do a little dance with it, and Kit follows me down the hallway as fast as her little legs will take her. I hear the door open and shut, and then it's just me and the baby. When she goes back into the living room, she notices her mom and dad are gone and she plops down on her bottom and lets out a long and disgusted wail.

I shake the toy and make faces at her, but it does no good. I drag her diaper bag over, trying to find something to take her mind off her parents, and she spies her bottle. She pulls it from a pouch on the side of the bag and pops into her mouth. She immediately quiets.

Well, I never saw a self-serve baby before. Maybe the rest of the day will be this easy.

Sam

I knock on the door and step back, about to shit my shorts in fear. Marta opens the door and looks up at me and grins. She motions me forward. "Is Emilio here?" I ask. I wipe my feet on the doormat.

She crosses her arms in front of her chest. She has flour on her cheek and her forehead is damp.

"Am I interrupting you?" I ask.

"Not at all." She motions for me to follow her to the kitchen. Emilio is there and he's icing cupcakes, grumbling to himself.

"Are you here to help?" he grouses.

"Um…" I straighten my spine. "Actually, I came to talk to you."

His eyes narrow.

Marta smiles at me, winks, and walks out of the room whistling.

"What do you want?" he asks. He blows out a breath.

He's struggling with a bag of icing. I motion for him to hand it to me. "What are these for?" I ask.

"Marta got a wild hair up her ass and decided she had to make several million of these little fuckers for the bake sale at the church." He grumbles obscenities. "The girls were supposed to help her, but Peck suddenly had something she had to do today, and the rest of them haven't shown up yet. So who gets drafted?" He points to his chest. "Me, that's who. And I fucking hate this shit." He glares at me. "What did you come here for?"

"Oh, nothing," I mutter.

He sets down the cupcake he's holding. "Nothing's wrong with Peck, is it?"

"No, she's fine."

I start to pipe icing onto a cupcake. Emilio watches me and grins. "You can stay," he says.

I laugh. "I'll stay. I have an hour before I have to be somewhere."

He takes another batch of cupcakes out of the oven. I've honestly never seen so many cupcakes in one place before. They're everywhere.

"So what brought you here?" Emilio asks.

I don't set the icing bag down, because it's nice to have something to do with my hands, although they're suddenly shaking. "I wanted to talk to you about Peck."

"What about her?"

"I wanted to see if you'd have any objections to me asking her to marry me."

I hear a whoop from the other room. Emilio rolls his eyes.

"Why do you want to marry her?"

Why *do* I want to marry her? She's just Peck. And I feel like she was made for me. "Um…"

"The answer is no, if that's the best you can do." He points to the cupcakes. "Ice them," he says.

I ice quietly for a few minutes, trying to gather my thoughts.

"Didn't expect you to give up quite so easily," he suddenly says.

I look up. "Oh, I'm not giving up. I'm just thinking."

"You about done with that?"

I shake my head. "Not yet."

"Keep icing."

Suddenly, Marta strolls into the room. There's purpose in her stride and I back up against the wall, because I'm afraid I'm her target. But I quickly see I'm not. She goes for Emilio, but he must be used to this. He runs around the corner of the center island and she chases him. She picks up a rolling pin and runs, but he runs a little bit faster. Suddenly, she stops and blows a stray lock of hair from her eyes. "Stop tormenting the poor boy," she says. She shakes the rolling pin at him.

"Oh, Jesus Christ," he breathes. "I was having fun with it!" He grins. Then he sobers completely. "Did Peck tell you about the day we met?"

"Yes, sir," I tell him.

"What she didn't tell you was my side of it." He rubs at the back of his hand. "I had been hanging out in the boys' ward at the home, and one of the little assholes bit me on the back of the hand, so I was in a bad mood. I wanted nothing more than to get out of there. I walked around the corner, trying to find Marta, and I saw her sitting beside a little girl. I took one look at that kid and I said to myself, *She's my daughter.*" He takes a deep breath. "I know it sounds stupid, and I suppose it should. But she was sitting there on the edge of the bed and she wouldn't speak. But when she looked at me, she said a million words with her eyes."

Marta wipes a tear from her cheek.

"I have loved that little girl from the minute I met her. I never doubted that she belonged to us, and neither did she."

He waits a beat.

"The first time she spoke to me was when she had a set of drumsticks in her hand." He looks at me. "Do you know what she said?"

I shake my head, and swallow past the lump in my throat.

"She took my hand and said, 'I'm glad you're my dad.' It was one big stutter, and I loved every syllable. She makes me so fucking proud." He points a finger at me. "She's fucking perfect, so if you so much as make her cry, I will find you and jam her drumsticks so far up your ass that you'll taste them ten years from now. Do you understand?"

"Yes, sir." I swallow again.

"So, yes, you can marry my daughter. And you better make her happy every day for the rest of her life, because I will be watching. Understand?"

"Yes, sir."

He points to the cupcakes. "Keep icing."

"Yes, sir." I grin.

Marta lays a hand on my shoulder. "Did you get a ring yet?"

"No, ma'am. I wanted to get permission first."

She looks at Emilio and quirks a brow. He nods.

She disappears into a bedroom and comes back a minute later with a box.

"It was my mother's," Emilio says. "Peck used to try it on all the time when she was small, and she loves it. So you can use it if you want to." He's grumbling, but I can tell he's serious.

I pop open the box and stare down at a beautiful antique ring. "It's lovely. Are you sure it's okay if I use it?"

He nods. He points to the cupcakes. "Keep icing."

"Yes, sir." I smile. I stay until the four remaining Zeroes get there, and then it becomes an estrogen-filled party. Emilio disappears into his office and I get out of there as quickly as I can.

***

I let myself into my apartment and stumble to a stop. Peck is lying on my couch, and she's not alone. She has a naked baby—well, naked except for a diaper and a pair of pink socks—sprawled across her chest. They're both asleep. Peck's hair is sticking out in every direction, and she's sweating where Kit is pressed against her neck.

Why on earth is Kit here with Peck? And where is Logan? He was MIA this morning and his daughter is here? What the fuck?

Kit has her thumb stuck in her mouth and she's sucking on it every few seconds.

I reach down and brush the hair from Peck's forehead. Her brown eyes blink open and she smiles softly at me.

"Hi," she whispers.

"Hi," I whisper back at her. "Why is Kit sleeping on you?"

"She got tired and started screaming, and she wouldn't stop. She cried until she made herself sick, so I changed her, and then she did it again, so I just left her naked." She lowers her chin to look down at the child. "She's adorable when she's sleeping, but the rest of the time, not so much."

"Why is she here?"

"Emily and Logan had somewhere they needed to go." She avoids my gaze.

"Where?"

She shrugs, but Kit stirs and she holds her breath. Kit's eyes fly open and she pushes up on her arms. Kit's cheeks are red and her face is damp and shiny where she's been drooling. Peck wipes her neck with her sleeve and grimaces.

"If she becomes nice just because you're here, I might have to throw you out the window. Just sayin'."

Kit grins at me and holds her arms out, so I take her and sit down with her on the other end of the couch. She sticks out a finger to point at Peck.

"I think she's hexing me," Peck grumbles.

"She likes you," I tell her. "She just doesn't know you well enough yet. She'll learn."

Kit has blond hair and blue eyes like Logan, and her two little hair bows are skewed from sleeping on my girlfriend.

"That's my girlfriend," I tell her.

Peck's eyes widen. "Is that what I am?" But she's smiling and blushing a little, so I think she's okay with my declaration.

"Yep. That's what you are." A grin tips the corners of my lips. "I feel like I should be passing you a note in class, one all folded up tight. *Will you be my girlfriend? Check yes or no.*"

Peck gets up on her knees and leans over me, pressing a quick kiss against my lips. "I would check the yes box," she tells me.

Kit rears back and slaps the side of her face.

"No!" I scold. And Kit's eyes fill up with tears.

"Oh, crap. You broke it," Peck mutters. She picks up a toy and shakes it in Kit's face, and Kit climbs from my lap to Peck's and starts to play. That'll last about thirty seconds, I figure.

"Where did you say Logan and Emily went?"

"I didn't." She sets Kit on the floor with her toy and gets up to get a drink. She comes back with two and hands me one. "How was your day?" she asks.

"It was fine." I'm not even going to tell her about how I'm planning to handle her mom's situation with Bone. I'd rather just do it and tell her about it later. It's easier to ask for forgiveness than to ask for permission.

I pat my pocket. I'm saving the ring for the right time.

I roll my shoulders. "I'm sore from today's workout with the trainer."

"Want me to rub your shoulders?" she asks.

I pull her to lie across me and kiss her forehead. "Maybe later."

She's quiet for a few minutes as Kit plays on the floor, and then she suddenly whispers, "You know, I'm leaving in two days. Six whole weeks away on tour."

I squeeze her a little tighter. "I know. I hate it." I lift her a little so I can look into her face. "Any chance your period will be done before you leave?" I whisper in her ear.

She tucks her face into my chest. I can feel her words, hot through my T-shirt. "Probably not."

I nudge her. "Are you blushing?"

She nods, her nose brushing my side.

"How many boyfriends have you had?"

She stiffens in my arms. "Why do you ask?"

"I'm just curious." I shake my head. "You don't have to tell me."

"Define boyfriend." She sits up, pushing her hair back behind her ear as she leans back on the other end of the couch. I lift her foot and pull it into my lap.

"Someone you hung out with, had meals with, spent time with, who was probably a man. With a penis."

"Well, I'd hope a man would have a penis." She grins.

I tug her toe until she squeals.

"Not many, if you're really curious. My numbers are pretty low."

I narrow my eyes at her. "I wasn't talking about sex."

"What's the difference?"

"We haven't had sex yet, and I consider you to be my girlfriend."

"What we're doing..." She motions from me to her and back. "...I've never done this before."

My heart swells a little, and I find it hard to take a deep breath all of a sudden. "Really?"

She nods.

"Good, because I feel the same way."

She blushes.

Suddenly, there's a knock on the door. Kit's head pops up and she runs toward it. "Ma ma ma ma ma," she babbles.

I pick her up and hold her while I open the door. Logan stands up a little straighter when he sees me. "What are you doing here?" he asks.

"I live here." I lean in the doorway. "Did you forget something here? Your keys, maybe?" I look down at Kit. "Oh!" I cry. "You forgot your kid."

He claps his hands and Kit jumps into his arms.

They walk in long enough to gather her things from all over the place, get her dressed, and then they get ready to leave. Logan is acting funny, and I have no idea why.

"You okay?" I ask him.

He nods. "We need to get home. We still have to finish packing."

Emily hugs Peck and they huddle together for a second. I hear the words *tomorrow* and *it'll be fine.*

"What's happening tomorrow?" I ask, as I follow them to the door.

Emily looks up at Logan and prompts him with her eyes.

"Nothing," he mumbles.

He flashes me the *I love you* sign and leans over so Kit can give me a kiss, and then he walks away.

"What was that all about?" I ask Peck.

She shrugs. "What are you making for dinner?" She grins at me, and dips her face into her shoulder like the question embarrassed her.

"What would you like?"

"Anything you want to make." She lifts her shirt and smells it. "But I need a shower, because I smell like a kid threw up on me over and over."

I walk close and sniff her. "You kind of do."

She scrunches up her face.

"Need help with your shower?" I grin at her and waggle my eyebrows.

"Not unless you're a glutton for punishment."

I kind of am. So I follow her to the bathroom. We aren't going to do anything. But I can touch her. And look at her. And just be with her. This having-a-girlfriend thing is pretty awesome.

Peck

The whole Reed clan shows up to see us off. I should have expected that, since Logan and Emily are going with us. But still, the Reeds *en masse* are a force that can be a little overwhelming. They're just so damn big and there are so many of them.

We're flying to Vegas, and then from there we pick up the tour and we'll be on a bus the rest of the travel. Two full weeks in Vegas, and then four more weeks of going all over the place. I'm excited, but I'm also apprehensive.

Logan and Emily arrive last at the airport. They get out of the car and Logan is wearing a toboggan. "Dude, what's up with the hat?" Pete asks him.

Logan ignores him. He has dark shadows under his eyes and I'm a little bit worried about him.

Sam shoots Pete a look, and I see Paul studying Logan hard. Logan ignores them, and keeps unloading the luggage from the car.

Sam pulls me against him and whispers in my ear. "The next time I see you, I'm going to fuck you so hard."

I choke.

Sam laughs as he pats me on the back, holding me tight against him. "Sorry, was that too graphic?" he asks me.

"I'll believe it when I see it."

He growls and kisses me.

Suddenly, someone shoves his shoulder and knocks him off balance. "Dude, you're in public," Matt says, but he's grinning.

My sisters watch as hugs go around the group, and Emilio and Marta bullshit with the Reeds right up until it's time to go through security.

Marta adjusts the neckline of my shirt and says, "Call me every day."

"I promise." I grin. I love that she's like this.

She wipes a tear from her eye, and Emilio grabs me and hugs me, swinging me around. "Love you, Woody," he says close to my ear.

"Love you too," I murmur back, my face stuck somewhere near his armpit. He does the same with my sisters, and until we all finally break free.

"This is way too much hugging," Lark says as the Reeds tell them goodbye, too.

Sam whispers something to Emilio and then Emilio steps back and hitches his hip against the wall. He grins. Something is up. I just don't know what.

"So," Sam says really loudly.

Friday is holding her phone up and she has the video on. What's going on?

I glare at Sam, because apparently I'm the only one who's not in on the joke. "What?" I ask him.

Then he pulls a box from his pocket and drops down on one knee in front of me. I cover my mouth with my hand.

He pops the top of the box and I see a great big diamond ring shining back at me. "So, you wanna?" he says.

"Do I wanna...?" I repeat. My heart is in my throat.

"Marry me, cupcake." He stares up at me, blinking those beautiful blue eyes.

"Now?" We're about to leave. I jerk my thumb toward the airport. I can't make any more words.

He laughs and shakes his head. "Not right this second, but soon. We can make little cupcakes together. You can be my plus-one. Or it can just be me and you. But you and me is not negotiable. I kind of need you, cupcake. Have ever since I met you."

I look down at him.

He adjusts his stance. "How much longer are you going to make me kneel here on my bad knee?" He grins at me.

"Oh, God!" I cry. I help him up and then I hold out my hand. "P-put it on me. I w-wanna."

My hand is shaking in the air, and he takes it in his and slides the ring onto my finger. That's when I realize it's Emilio's mother's ring. I look at him and he shrugs and smiles.

Then Sam picks me up and spins me around. I'm dizzy when he finally sets me down and I cling to him.

Cameras snap all around us, and I bury my face in Sam's chest. He laughs and holds me close. "You sure?" he asks me quietly, so only I can hear.

"More sure than I have ever been of anything." And I mean it. I really do.

Emilio gives me one last hug.

"Did you know about this?" I ask him.

He shrugs. "He came to see me yesterday to ask me for permission."

"And?"

"And he just asked you, didn't he?" He chuckles. "He's a good one." Emilio brushes a lock of hair back from my forehead. "I wouldn't let just anyone marry one of my daughters. Particularly not the first one I ever had."

My eyes fill with tears and I blink them back furiously.

Sam gives me one last kiss and I wave at him until I can't see him anymore. This time, I don't want to see him as a speck in the distance. It's not where he needs to stay. Not now. Not ever.

Logan sits down in a chair in the waiting area and puts his head in his hands.

"Is he okay?" I ask Emily.

She nods. But then she shakes her head. "He should have told them, and now he wishes he did. But he can't, because now it would hurt their feelings."

Logan jerks the toboggan off his head and jams it into his backpack. Then he picks up his daughter and sets her on his knee.

The longer Logan waits to tell them, the harder it will be.

Sam

It has been a week and a half since Peck left. We talk every day on the phone, and we use Face Time as much as we can. But I'm going crazy without her. I get my boot off next week, and then I'll go back to training full time. I'm both excited and apprehensive about it.

I worked at the shop all day today, and I'm cleaning my station. I roll my shoulders, because they're tense. I know what I'm going to do tonight carries some risk, but it needs to be done, and I'm not going to leave it to Peck to do it. Nor am I going to take any of my brothers into it with me.

Everyone is gone but me and Josh, and I turn the lights off and put the money in the safe. I take out the package with ten thousand dollars in cash in it, which I put in here earlier today, and stuff it into the pocket of my hoodie. Josh follows me to the door and I open it so he can roll through.

"You have plans tonight?" I ask.

He shakes his head. "No."

"What do you do when you leave here, man?" I ask. I'm a nosy bastard. I can't help it.

"Nothing much."

I nod and say, "Good night, then."

He rolls in the other direction without a word.

I shrug my shoulders and start down the street. Bone's office is a few streets over, so I can walk there.

But as I get close to the fence that surrounds his building, I see Paul leaning against the fence. He has one boot heel pressed against the fence, his knee bent. I know he looks relaxed to everyone else, but he's not relaxed at all to me. He's seething.

"Are you stupid?" he fires off.

"Why are you here?" I ask.

"Did you really think we were going to let you go in there alone?"

Matt walks up beside us.

"Not you too," I groan, letting my head fall back.

"You get all of us, except for Logan." He puts a hand on my shoulder and squeezes. "And we promised to call him as soon as this is over."

"I'm not taking you in there with me."

"You're not going alone," Pete says.

"Fuck all of you." I say it, but there's no heat in my voice, and they know it.

"Well, let's go," Paul says. "We need to go see the drug-dealing whoremonger now, because we have kids we need to get home to." He arches a brow at me.

"Exactly why you should stay here." I march past them all, and they walk right behind me. "Do you listen to anything I say?"

"Where you go, we go," Paul says.

I blow out a breath and ring the bell outside Bone's office. I've been here before. It was back when Pete and I worked for him, but it has been a while. Someone opens the door and I tell him what I want. The door shuts in my face, and I hear feet move down the hallway. Then the door opens again and the guy motions us forward.

He and two other guys frisk us all. He gets way too close to my balls and I sidestep to get away from his questing fingers. "Hey!" I cry.

He shrugs and motions us into Bone's office.

The man himself is sitting behind a huge cherry desk. The walls are heavy dark-wood paneling, and he looks supremely satisfied to see me.

"Well, look who's here," he sings out.

His guys go to stand on each side of the desk. There are three of them. They're big and they're packing.

I stick out my hand and Bone shakes it. "I came to talk to you about my girlfriend's mother." I pull the money out of the pocket of my hoodie. "I want to make good on her debt."

He takes the package and hands it to one of his guys, who proceeds to count it. "Ten thousand, boss," he says.

Bone shakes his head. "Not enough."

"How much more do you need?" I'll get him whatever he wants. But I really need to get my brothers out of here before someone gets hurt.

"Ten more."

"Okay. I'll get it."

Bone nods. He sucks his gold teeth for a minute and says, "You look like him, you know that?"

Beside me, Paul goes even stiffer than he was.

"Like who?" I ask.

"Your dad." He laughs. But it's not amusing. Not at all. He picks up a pen and sights down the middle of it like he's lining up a shot. Then he pretends to fire. "I never saw anyone cry quite as much as your dad did."

"What?" Paul barks.

"When I killed him. Before I stuffed him into the freezer, at least. He was still alive when I left him. Though I doubt it was for long."

"Why?" Paul asks.

"Wrong place, wrong time," Bone says. He shrugs like it's nothing.

Before I even know what's happening, Paul jumps.

Everything after that second happens like it's in slow motion. Paul flies over the top of the desk and grabs Bone by the throat.

Pete knocks one of the guys to the ground, and his gun skitters across the floor.

Matt grabs another and flips him over onto his stomach. I throw a sucker punch at the last one standing.

It's melee. Nothing but pandemonium. I hear Paul's fists flying, and the crunch of knuckles against bones. The grunts of my brothers as they struggle with anyone who would get in Paul's way.

Suddenly, time freezes. It's like my mother's old record player when it would scratch across a forty-five. *Screech!* The crack of gunshot vibrates the air around us and everyone stops moving.

Paul is the first one to step back. He stands up with his hands in the air. The others do the same.

One of Bone's guys reaches for his gun and Josh yells out, "Leave it!" He points the barrel of his nine-millimeter squarely at Bone's sidekick. The guy freezes.

"Well, look who else came to the party." Bone lies on the floor and laughs. His words gurgle and he turns his head to spit out a mouthful of blood. His face is a bloody mess, but he's laughing. He rolls his head onto its side so he can look at Josh. Josh reaches down and locks the wheels of his chair with one hand. His other hand is steady.

"Don't move," Josh says to the others. He motions for me and my brothers to come toward him with a jerk of his head.

"Don't do anything stupid," Paul says.

"You first," Josh responds. He doesn't take his eyes off Bone's men. Or Bone. It's like watching his eyes follow a ping-pong match. "Get out of here." He jerks his head toward the door again.

"What are you going to do?" Matt asks.

Josh laughs. "I'm leaving with you."

Suddenly Bone moves, and he lifts a gun from beneath his desk where he fell. I watch as he raises it, and I know exactly when Josh realizes it.

The blast from a gun shot in close quarters cracks hard, like a firecracker inside a glass bottle. The room shivers with the burst of it. Or that might just be my fear. I'm not sure which it is. We all fall to the ground, except for Josh. So I grab him and knock him from the chair, taking him down with us.

The room goes silent. Bone's men look over at him and then they run out the door. "Oh, fuck," Paul says.

"That wasn't what I planned on doing," Josh says. He shoves my shoulder. "Would you get off me?"

I roll off of him and he adjusts his legs and pulls himself back up into the chair.

"Is he dead?" Paul asks.

I walk over to Bone and see that he has a single shot wound directly through the center of his forehead. "He's dead," I confirm. I kick his shoulder just to be sure. I half expect him to reach and grab my leg or something, but he's dead. Dead as a doornail.

"Fuck," Paul breathes as he swipes a hand down his face.

Matt is already dialing 9-1-1.

The police show up and it takes hours for everyone to tell their stories. It's late by the time we get back home. We all go to Paul's, where the wives and kids are waiting. I swear, when we get there I'm afraid Friday is going to slap the shit out of Paul, after he tried to tell her about it all on the phone.

Then we have to hash over it again. And again.

"I can't believe that really happened. What would have happened if Josh hadn't been there?" Friday asks.

Josh is locked up, at least for now. Reagan is already calling her dad to get him to go see him, to see if he needs or wants a kick-ass criminal attorney.

"I don't know," Paul says.

"When you jumped over that fucking desk…" Matt growls.

"I know." He picks PJ up and holds him close. "I know," he whispers.

I look around the room and see my brothers, all of whom have the women they love supporting them.

"I need to go see Peck," I suddenly blurt out.

"Okay," Paul says slowly, drawing the word out so that it lasts forever.

"I'll give you a ride to the airport," Pete says.

"I'll take a cab." I flash them all one big *I love you* sign and run out the door. I don't even stop at my apartment for clothes. I go straight to the airport, where I catch the last flight out for Vegas.

I need her. I need her like she's the air I breathe.

***

When I get to the stadium, they won't let me in the staff entrance, so I have to call Logan and have him come get me. He walks up with Kit in his arms, and hands me a pass to hang around my neck. Kit is wearing a pair of noise cancelling headphones on her ears, and she doesn't appear to like them very much.

"Are you okay?" he asks.

"Did you talk to Paul?"

He scowls at me. "So Paul went off on him, huh?"

I growl. "The moment he started talking about how he left Dad alive in that freezer, Paul jumped over the desk and grabbed him by the throat." I shake my head. "Scared the shit out of me."

"I wish I had been there."

I'm glad he wasn't, but I sort of wish he had been. "Do you know where Peck is?"

He walks down a long hallway and through a set of doors. The floor is vibrating with the beat of the music, and my feet shake.

He points onto the stage.

I see her.

She's sitting on a stool with her sticks in her hand, and she's playing for all she's worth. Her hair is wet, and when she shakes her head, drops of water fly in every direction.

She's wearing a T-shirt with the arms cut out, and I can see her upper arms, toned from years of playing the drums. She may worry about other parts of her body, but she shouldn't worry about her arms. Or any of the rest of her, as far as I'm concerned, because she's fucking perfect.

And she's mine.

Emily walks off the stage and comes toward Logan. "Let's go talk," she says.

I point to Peck. "I want to talk to her."

I'm nearly shaking with need. I need her. I need to hold her, to have her touch me. I need her. Just her.

"She's going to be at least another hour." Emily nods toward the exit.

I follow, because they start walking without waiting for me.

We walk into a quiet room that has a star and Emily's name on it. Logan takes Kit's headphones off, and she stops struggling with them.

"Tell us what happened," Emily says. She sits down. She's sweaty too, but nothing like Peck was.

I start at the beginning and tell them everything.

Peck

We're done. Finally. Thank God. Because after a performance like that, I always feel like my arms are going to fall off.

The crowd is going nuts, and we already did an encore. We have to be finished now. The venue management is motioning for us to call it quits, so we take a final bow and walk off the stage.

There's another group, a small-time act, that played before we did, and their drummer has been hitting on me ever since we got here. Apparently, he started drinking as soon as their set was over, because the smell of liquor wafts across the room toward me. I wave my hand in front of my face.

I make a move to walk by him to go to our dressing room, and an arm suddenly snakes around my waist. I squeal as he jerks me against him and touches his lips to mine. The photogs that are allowed backstage go crazy taking pictures. I push back from him, and he doesn't stop, so I slap him. The noise rings out around the room.

He jerks back like I just hurt his feelings. Then he sneers.

"What's the m-m-matter?" he mocks. "You l-l-looked like you could use a k-k-kiss."

I start toward him with my fist raised, because I'm going to punch him in the fucking throat. But Star gets between me and him. I reach around her, but she holds me back. "Get out of the way, Star," I warn.

She nods toward security, but before they can get there, Fin—the tiniest out of our group of five—tugs on the guy's sleeve. He looks down at her, his eyes filled with lascivious intent. "Hey, baby," he croons.

He bends down like he wants to try his luck kissing her, but she balls up her fist and hits him square in the nose. He falls back, completely stunned, and lands on his back in the middle of the floor. Star steps in the center of his chest and presses the heel of her boot into his breastbone. "If you ever fucking touch one of my sisters again, I'll chop your balls off and feed them to you."

Our security guy loops a hand around Fin's waist and picks her up, putting her behind him, while another scoops the drummer up off the floor.

"Get him off our tour," Star says. "I never want to see him again."

"Yes, ma'am," the operations manager for the tour says. He wipes his brow with a handkerchief.

Fin shakes out her hand. "That really hurt." She winces.

"You should have let me deck him."

"We need your hands more than we need mine." She grins. "By the way, you can't have all the fun." She chucks my shoulder with hers, then looks at a spot over my shoulder and smirks. "Speaking of fun..."

Another fucking arm snakes around my middle, but this time I'm prepared. I let whoever it is spin me around, and then I throw a punch just like Emilio taught me to. The heel of my hand hits him straight in the nose and he jerks back, holding his hand to his face.

"Fuck!" he cries.

"Oh, that was *awesome*," Logan says. He high-fives Emily and she's almost bent over laughing.

"God, cupcake..."

"Sam?" I say.

He looks up. "Nice to see you too," he says. Someone presses a towel into his hands, and he wipes his nose.

"Oh my God," I cry. I grab his forearms and try to pull them away from his nose. "I'm so sorry. I didn't know it was you. I thought it was the asshole."

"What asshole?" Sam pulls the towel back and a thin trickle of blood runs down from his nose.

"Never mind," I say. I pull his arms down and look into his eyes. "Are you really here?"

He nods. "I would say that the blood confirms it."

I jump against him and wrap my arms around his neck. He puts his arms around me and holds me close, despite the fact that I just hit him in the nose. "I can't believe you're here." I pull back and look into his face. "Is everything okay?" I ask.

"It is now," he says, and then he kisses me.

Sam

Facing death makes you eager to prove you're alive.

I start pulling her clothes off as soon as we get into the hotel room, before the door is even closed. I grab the tail of her shirt, which is wringing with sweat, and pull it over her head. She's wearing a purple bra, and I stop to stare at her tits. I lick my lips and she covers them with her hand.

"No fucking way," I tell her, and I grab her arms to pull them down.

Her cheeks are blazing red and I know she's not comfortable naked, so I kiss her. I kiss her like there's no tomorrow. Like we'll never get to kiss again.

And she responds the same way.

"I need a shower," she says. She scrunches up her face. "I'm sweaty."

"Later," I say. I reach behind her and unhook her bra. Then I slow things down and pull the straps down her shoulders and off. The wires of her bra hold it up, and she covers it with her hands to keep it from falling off.

I reach for the waist of her jeans and unbutton them, since her hands are busy holding up her bra.

I shove them, along with her panties, down over her hips, and then I kiss her as I walk her back toward the bed. "Next time, we'll do this slowly. But I can't wait."

"Okay," she says against my lips. Her tongue tangles with mine, until I push her back on the bed. She sits down, and I unbutton my jeans and start to slide them down, but she grabs my ass and pulls me down on top of her. "Now," she says.

I reach down between her legs, because I need to be sure she's as ready as I am. She's slick and wet and so hot. I pull a condom from my back pocket, which is now down around my knees, tear it open with my teeth, and roll it on.

I swipe past her clit and she sifts her fingers through my hair, pulling gently. She spreads her thighs wide, and I settle between them. My pants are half on and half off, and I don't care. I couldn't get them down over my boot without a lot of work, anyway. I sink inside her in one harsh thrust.

She cries out.

"Are you okay?" I look into her face. Her eyes are closed, her mouth hangs open, and tiny little breaths fall onto my cheek like humid raindrops.

"Don't stop," she says.

She grabs my ass and pulls me into her. The musky scent of her sweat tickles my nose, and I lick the salt from the side of her neck. She lets go of the bra, and I pull it away with my teeth, and look down at her tits. I wrap my lips around one of her nipples and give it a tug as I press as far inside her as I can go. I hold it, grinding into her.

"God, you feel so good."

"Fuck me, Sam. Hard. Please."

She rocks her hips and takes me deeper. I can't wait. I can't. I want to make this last, but I can't. My balls are already trying to crawl up my throat.

I sit up a little and push her right leg against her chest, and put my weight on it. I can see myself sinking inside her from this angle, my dick all shiny and wet. I spread her lower lips and find her clit. It's swollen and round and my thumb slides across it. She stops pushing against me and stills. "Yeah," she breathes.

I push in and pull out in quick, deep strokes. She cries out my name. "Sam!"

"Oh God, Peck," I say. "God, you feel so good. I can't stop."

She squeezes my dick when she comes. I stop, and enjoy the little flutters of her pussy squeezing me tightly, like a hot, wet fist. She rocks against my hand, and I let her ride out her orgasm, watching her face closely. I've never seen anything so beautiful. So right. So mine.

"I need to come," I plead. I wanted to make this last at least thirty seconds, but that's not going to happen.

She freezes. I take my weight off her leg and she lowers it. I don't know what she wants for me to do. I'm going to marry this woman. I know that.

"Come, Sam," she growls in my ear. "Come for me now."

I wrap my arms under her shoulders so I can power into her, pressing as hard as I can go, as deep as I can get. She holds me close, her arms wrapped around me as I let go deep inside her.

I've never come so hard in my life. I feel like part of me is pouring into her. My heart. My brain. My center. *Me.*

"God, I love you so much," I say, as I collapse on top of her. She tangles her fingers in my hair and scratches my scalp with her fingernails. I'm spent. I don't even have enough energy to roll off of her. "God, I didn't know it was going to be like that," I tell her quietly.

She jerks under me. "What do you mean?"

"I mean that was the best, most explosive fucking orgasm I have ever had. I thought the top of my head was going to blow off."

She laughs, and it pushes my softening dick out of her. I lift my head and kiss the tip of her nose.

Her cheeks are rosy and she's suddenly fidgety. "You okay?" I ask.

"Yeah." She smiles softly up at me. "I'm okay. Now that you're here, I'm fine. I really missed you." She squeezes my arm. "Why are you here?"

"Well, I almost died, and when I didn't, I realized the only thing I wanted was you, so here I am."

She shoves my shoulder so I have no choice but to roll off of her. She jerks the edge of the blanket to cover herself. "*What?*"

I heave a sigh. "It's a long story."

"Then you had better start telling it."

I dispose of the condom and spend the next half hour telling her all about my afternoon. She's appropriately wounded, offended, relieved, and grateful. She lies quietly beside me when my story is over.

"Thanks for doing that," she says. "For me. You didn't have to."

"I'd do just about anything for you."

"Well, if you ever do anything that stupid again, I might have to kill you myself."

She lies there for a long while without saying a word.

"Hey, cupcake!" I say, like I just had a great idea.

She laughs. "Hey, Sam."

"We need to get married."

She lifts her head. "What?"

"We're in Vegas. We can get married by an Elvis impersonator." I press my hands together like I'm praying. "Pretty please," I beg.

She laughs again. I don't think she's aware that I'm serious.

"I'm *serious*. Totally." I stare into her dark eyes.

"Why?"

I start to tick items off on my fingers. "One—I love you. Two—I don't want to be apart from you anymore. Three—we just had sex, and if you refuse to marry me, I'll think you just used me for my body." I snake a hand beneath the covers and lay it on her belly. "Not that I'm complaining." I tick off one more item. "And four—you punched me in the nose, so you have to marry me. It's a rule."

She giggles. "It is, huh?"

"Yep. So, what do you say?" I toss the covers back and press my lips to her belly. She holds my head there for a second, and then her belly jiggles with laughter.

"Can I shower first?"

I look up and see that she's grinning at me. "Seriously?" I ask.

She nods. "Yeah."

I jump to my feet and dig my phone out of my pants pocket. My pants are still hanging around my shins, which is kind of embarrassing, so I hitch them higher. I call Logan and put him on Face Time. *Dude, I need a best man*, I sign to him.

"What?" he asks, his voice groggy.

I need a best man. I'm so fucking excited that I can barely sit still.

"Give us thirty minutes," he says.

I get ready to hand Peck my phone, but she has already fished hers out and is talking to one of her sisters. I can hear multiple squeals on the other end of the line. She holds the phone out and curses. "Thirty minutes," she says. She nods, and then she gets up and dashes into the bathroom to take a shower.

I go with her, just because I like the sight of her ass naked, and all the rest of her too, not to mention that it's about to be mine for eternity.

***

It's almost four in the morning by the time she comes out of the bathroom. I went in there and showered with her, but it just made me want her again, so I climbed out and got dressed. I don't have anything to wear aside from what I wore here, so I'm feeling a little out of sorts. Particularly when she comes out of the bathroom wearing a dress, some strappy silver sandals, and her hair has been blown out and styled. She's wearing a little makeup, too.

I grab her and growl into her neck. "Damn, you look good enough to eat."

She laughs and shoves me away. "Maybe later."

I scratch my chin. "I wonder if it's any different eating out your wife."

She blinks her pretty brown eyes at me. "I don't have a wife."

I laugh out loud. "God, I love you."

A knock sounds on the door and I open it to find Logan leaning in the doorway. He has a nice outfit hooked on a hanger over his shoulder. I recognize it. It's one of the ones Emily's mom gets from Madison Avenue, the clothing line they own. It's classy. And really great. "You didn't buy this, did you?"

He shakes his head. "I brought it just in case."

"Just in case I got married?"

"Just in case we had to go somewhere nice on the tour." He shakes his head and grins. "Just put it on and shut up."

"Where's Em?" I ask.

"She had to wake Kit up and get her dressed."

Oh, fuck. I totally forgot about how much this would inconvenience them. "Tell her to go back to bed. I didn't mean to mess up your whole night."

He scoffs. "Are you kidding? She wouldn't miss it. And she's going to hold the camera for the rest of the crew."

"What crew?"

"Your brothers. Pete? Matt? Paul?"

"They're awake?"

"They are now. They're waiting to see you tie the knot."

My heart swells in my chest and I have to swallow past the lump in my throat.

"Go get dressed," Logan says.

I go in the bathroom and change clothes. I can't hear him talking with Peck, which means they're either standing there looking stupid at one another or they're signing. My bet is that they're signing. I just wish I knew what they're talking about.

I walk back out and point to my feet. I have no nice shoes. Logan toes his own black tennis shoes off and kicks them toward me. I throw mine at him and he slides them on his feet.

There's a squeal on the other side of the door and a rapid knock. Peck opens the door to her sisters, and they swarm her all at once.

When they finally let her go, I take her hand in mine. "You ready to go get married?" I ask.

She nods, chewing on her lower lip. "I'm ready," she says quietly.

There's one thing I know for sure. I am the luckiest man in the world.

Peck

Sam takes my breath away. He's dressed in a blue button-down shirt that makes his eyes even bluer than normal, and black pants. We walk to the first drive-through marriage convenience center we see, and they do have an Elvis impersonator to perform the ceremony, so Sam is happy. They sell him a package, including rings for the two of us, flowers for me to hold, and they give us petals for Kit to toss, although she tries to eat them all first.

When the owner of the chapel finds out we're Skyping all the family in, he hooks our phone up to his big screen, so we can see them all. They're all at their own houses, but the screen is split so we have Matt and Sky, Paul and Friday, Reagan and Pete, and Marta and Emilio on conference call. I see one extra box on the screen. I lean toward it and say, "Who is that?"

Sam grins. "Henry."

I wave. "Hi, Henry!"

He waves back.

"I can't believe we're doing this," I murmur to Sam.

His eyes narrow. "You don't want to?"

"No, no! I do." But I point to the Elvis impersonator and laugh. "But this guy…"

Sam chuckles.

Elvis starts to sing "Viva Las Vegas" as Sam and I walk side by side down the aisle. I cover my mouth and laugh.

"I want you to repeat after me, Sam," Elvis says. He lifts one corner of his lip in that classic snarl. "I, Sam, promise you, Peck, never to step on your blue suede shoes. I promise never to leave you at Heartbreak Hotel. I promise to be your hunka-hunka burning love, forever and ever, amen."

"Wait," Sam says. "That's Randy Travis. Not Elvis."

"Close enough," Elvis says.

Sam rolls his hips like Elvis did when he repeats the words.

I can't stop laughing. I laugh so hard that I have to wipe tears from my eyes. But I don't feel bad, because Emily is doing the same thing. And the rest of the brothers and their wives are laughing it up too.

"Now you, Peck," Elvis says. He swivels his hips and someone does a rim shot on a set of drums. "I, Peck, solemnly swear to love you tender for the rest of my life, and never leave you with a suspicious mind."

I repeat the words. I barely stutter, and it warms my heart when I realize that.

Suddenly, Elvis gets serious. "Dearly beloved, we are gathered here today..."

Sam's eyes meet mine, and he takes my hands. I pass my flowers to one of my sisters and look up at him. We recite the official vows, and I have to blink hard to get through them, particularly when I look at the TV screen and see Marta crying into her handkerchief.

"Who gives this woman to be married?" Elvis asks.

Emilio's voice rings out. "Her mother and I."

This time, a hot tear tracks down my cheek and Sam very gently wipes it away. "You okay?" he whispers.

"I now pronounce you husband and wife," Elvis declares. "Now let's have a little less conversation and a really big kiss." He swivels his hips again and I laugh through my tears.

Sam pushes my hair from my neck and wraps his hand solidly around it, and pulls me to him. He kisses me long, deep, and I feel like it might go on forever. And I'm fine with that.

But then Emilio coughs into his fist. I hear him say, "Enough," over his hacking, and Sam pulls back with a grin.

"I couldn't help it," he whispers.

Elvis congratulates us and makes his exit, because he has a ceremony to perform next door. "You can stay and talk with your family for a few minutes if you want to," a lady tells us.

Sam pulls up a chair and then draws me into his lap. We face the screen as we accept congratulations from his family and from mine.

This feels like a dream. It feels like I'm going to wake up tomorrow and it'll all be over. But I want it to be real. Forever.

Marta and Emilio sign off, and so does Henry. My sisters are yawning, so I send them to bed too, with promises that we're almost done here. The brothers linger, though, and I wouldn't expect any less of them. It may be almost morning, but they're a unit, and I'm so happy Sam has a family like this.

Suddenly, Logan pulls his cap off and faces the screen. "Can I talk to you guys about something?" he says. He's signing while he's talking, and Paul signs back.

"Of course. What's up?" Paul tilts his screen so that it looks like he's closer.

Logan looks at Sam and signs *sorry*. Sam just furrows his brow and looks at Logan's head, directly behind his ear. He can clearly see where his hair was shaven for his implant. Sam looks at me, confusion clouding his face.

"Right before we left..." Logan begins. He has to stop and clear his throat. "Right before we left, I went and got a cochlear implant."

He stops talking, and I can see his eyes moving from one house to the other on the monitor. No one says a word. Not even Sam.

"I didn't tell you because I was afraid you'd try to stop me. And then I didn't tell you because I was afraid you *wouldn't* try to stop me. I was really afraid to do it, but it was something I really wanted. Something I really needed."

"Why didn't you tell us?" Paul asks. Everyone else is quiet.

"I just felt like I was betraying myself. And all of you. And I didn't like it. But I needed to do it." He clears his throat again. "I'm sorry I didn't tell you and I hope you can forgive me."

"Why are you telling us now?"

He jerks a thumb toward Sam. "I wanted to ruin his perfect wedding." He laughs, but it's a watery sound. He closes his eyes and waits a beat. "So, I was wondering... When we get home, they're going to activate this thing... And I was...kind of hoping...I was hoping you all could go with me when they do it." He takes a deep breath, and it's almost like he sucks all the air out of the room. I feel like there's an elephant sitting on my chest.

"Of course we'll go with you," Paul says quietly. "We wouldn't let you do it alone."

Logan hugs Emily against his side, and she has Kit in her arms. "I'm never alone. But I'd like it a whole lot better if you could all be there with me." His voice cracks. "I kind of need you guys. All of you."

Paul holds up the *I love you* sign. And although none of the brothers can see one another, they're all doing it at once. A sob forms in my chest, and I have to swallow it back. I wipe my eyes.

Pete sits back and scratches his belly. "Well, Sam needs to go get laid, so we're going to sign off."

Sam chuckles and pulls me closer, his hand on my hip. I put my arm around his shoulders.

"Even though I couldn't get laid on my wedding night because of my brother, I wouldn't want him to miss out." He scowls at Sam, until Reagan pops the back of his head. "Ow," he complains. Pete grows serious. "Congratulations, you two," Pete says. "We love you." His box disappears from the screen. One by one, they all send their well wishes. Paul is last, and he sends his love and a warning. "Use a condom, numb nuts," he says. Then he vanishes, too.

Logan scratches his head and looks sheepishly at Sam. "I'm really sorry."

Sam lifts me off his lap so that he can get up and look behind Logan's ear. "So that's all it is?" he asks.

"Until it gets activated, yeah."

"Cool." Sam takes my hand. "I can't wait to see how it works."

Logan heaves out a relieved sigh. "You don't think they're mad at me, do you?"

Sam shakes his head. "No. Maybe a little confused, though."

"Sorry I took your spotlight."

Sam's hand squeezes mine. "I got all the spotlight I need."

Peck

Sam takes my hand as we walk back to the hotel. The lights of the city are bright, and the sun is about to rise. The sky is waking with purples and oranges and we stop to look at it.

"Beautiful, isn't it?"

Sam brushes my hair back behind my ear. "Yes, you are."

Heat creeps up my cheeks. I'll never get used to this. Ever.

I cover my mouth with my hand when I yawn.

"When does your bus leave?" he asks.

"Ten in the morning."

"We had better get back to the room so you can get some sleep."

I lift a brow at him. "I can sleep on the bus."

"Are Logan and Emily going to be on your bus?"

I nod. "They get the only bedroom."

His brow furrows.

"It's set up kind of like rows of bunk beds, and there's one room in the back that has a full bed. They get that, since there are three of them. The rest of us get bunks."

"Well, that kind of sucks."

I laugh. "I don't mind. If they didn't take it, Fin would use it for whatever random hookup she found. At least this way, they can get some privacy. And maybe some sleep, too."

He makes a crude gesture with his hands. "Maybe some sex, too." He grabs me and pulls me against him. "Speaking of sex, we have a wedding night to get to." He growls against my neck and starts to nibble my skin. Heat shoots straight to the center of me.

"Race you," I whisper against his ear.

"I can't run, but you can. I need to stop at the convenience store, anyway." He waggles his brows at me playfully.

"Oh," I breathe out as heat creeps up my cheeks.

"Yeah," he says, and then he kisses me.

"I kind of need some time alone, anyway."

"For what?" He grins at me.

"You'll see."

He kisses me quickly and walks inside the hotel with me. He puts me in the elevator and I watch the doors close around his smile.

I'm feeling as out of place as a fart in church, which is weird because it's not like we haven't already been intimate.

I walk into my room and stop. On the bed lies a package. I pick up the note and see Fin's chicken scratch.

Thought you could use this. Don't worry—it's new. Never worn. Never sullied. So go dirty it up. Love you—Us.

I open the box and a bright red nightie falls out. It's long enough that it might fall to my upper thigh, and it has spaghetti straps with lace edging the top. It's pretty. And not slutty at all, so I know Fin didn't buy it for herself. She has a thing for lingerie though, so she could have bought it for any one of us. I guess I'm the lucky one.

I take it into the bathroom with me, and get in the shower. I take all the care I didn't have time to take earlier, shaving appropriate places and washing others. I get out and look at myself in the mirror. My hair is still dry, so I let it fall from the impromptu ponytail I put it in, and it lands around my shoulders. I wipe beneath my eyes to remove any mascara smudges that might be there, but I'm in pretty good shape, considering all the crying I did during the ceremony.

I still can't believe I married him. Or that he married me.

I'm just about the luckiest girl in the world.

I hear the outer door open and I take in a deep breath. I drop the slinky nightie over my head and adjust it so that it fits right on my boobs. I wish they were a little perkier, or a little less round. But Sam seems to like them.

I take a deep breath and open the door to the bathroom. I peek out and see Sam lying in the center of the bed with nothing on but his boxers. He has even taken the boot off his foot.

"Can you switch the l-light off?" I ask.

"Nope," he says. "I want to see everything." He sits up and hangs his legs off the edge of the bed. "Come here," he says gently.

I walk into the room, my knees shaking, my legs like Jell-o. I cross my arms in front of me, but then I remember the length of my nightie and I reach down to tug it a little bit over my thigh. But that makes the bodice dip, and so I have to tug it higher. I growl and give up. I flop down on the bed beside him and fall back. I can feel the material sliding up my thighs, giving him a huge view of my thighs. I cover my face with my arms and groan.

"You look so beautiful," he says. It's almost like a prayer. His hand lies flat on my stomach. I uncover my face.

"Do you like it?" I ask. "The Zeroes gave it to me."

"Why do you call yourselves that?" he asks. He turns so that he's facing me, and his hand skims my body. Goose flesh erupts on my arms and my nipples get hard. He sees it and licks his lips.

"It's something we started when we got to the group home. Lark and Wren were there first, and they were the Double Zeroes, because their room number was 10 but the one was missing on the door." The memory of it makes me smile. "They didn't really want me in their room, but they didn't have a choice."

"So, all of you became the Zeroes?" He sweeps a hand beneath my breast, and my breath hitches.

"Zero is rock bottom. We had Zip. Zero. Zilch. And we felt like we'd all fallen from zero. We were about as low as we could go."

"Then you met Emilio and Marta?"

I nod. "First there was Mrs. Derricks, though. She was the guidance counselor at my school."

"I knew her. She helped a lot with Pete's mentor program. That's why we were at her funeral that day."

"She saved my life."

"I'm glad she did," he says quietly. He drags his fingers down my thigh and hooks the hem of my nightgown. He draws it forward, his gaze hot as he uncovers me. I lift my hips as he goes higher and he stops and stares at me. "Damn, that's pretty," he growls.

I hold completely still, except for my heaving chest and my thumping heart.

He dips a finger into my folds and slides it down. I part my thighs for him ever so slightly. "So wet," he says. He strokes my clit, making small circles.

He's still sitting next to me, so I reach for his waistband. I pull it down, and his dick bobs up toward his belly button.

I sit up a little and push him onto his back. "Okay…" he says slowly, throwing up his hands. I lean over him and he gathers my hair into his fist, holding it so he can watch me.

A bead of pre-come forms on the head of his dick, and I take it into my mouth, letting the salty essence of him spread across my tongue. He makes a noise, and I see him close his eyes and bite his lower lip. "God, you're going to kill me," he swears.

I don't say anything. I take him further into my mouth, and wrap my hand around the base of his dick, pumping as I take him all the way to the back of my throat. He pushes forward, urging me to take a little more. I gag and he pulls back.

"Sorry," he mutters, but his feet are jiggling, so I do it again.

A hot flash of come shoots across my tongue and I swallow, but suddenly he grabs me and pulls me on top of him. He adjusts me so that I straddle him, and then he reaches between us to roll on a condom. I watch him and wonder what I'm supposed to do next. I have never been on top, and I'm not sure I want to be.

"I want to watch you," he tells me. He lifts me so that I'm leaning over him and he kisses me. I feel him nudge against my heat, and the head of his dick slips inside. I gasp against his lips, and he puts his hands on my hips and pushes in a little farther. "Sit up a little."

I sit up and I slide all the way down on him. A burst of pleasure shoots straight to my center and I gasp.

His hands lift the edge of my nightgown, and he hesitates, searching my eyes, asking for permission. I grab the end of it and yank it over my head. I am naked in so many ways. It's so much more than just being undressed, and he knows that, if the look in his eyes is any indication.

He cups my breasts in his hands and his thumbs track across the turgid peaks. He lifts them gently, and he moves inside me. I get it. I rise and fall, taking him all the way to the base. I can feel him deep inside.

Very slowly, I lift and take him to the very edge, and then I sink back down on him. He groans and closes his eyes, but his hands don't stop their wicked moves. My breasts ache, and my whole body trembles.

Sam lowers his hand to my curls and parts my sensitive flesh. My legs falter as he strums my clit, and I have to brace myself with the palm of his hand on my chest. "Don't stop," he urges.

He pumps his hips, meeting my every fall, and countering my every retreat.

My movements grow shaky, and I'm not sure I can do this much longer, but suddenly pleasure flashes in the center of me, and I come. I press down with both hands on his chest and ride the wave, gasping as my body convulses, until I can't take anymore and I fall, weak and spent, onto his chest.

He strokes my back, still thick and hot inside me, spearing to the very center of me.

He rolls us over so that I land on the quilt, and then he flips me onto my tummy. I'm like a ragdoll at this point, so weak and warm that he could do just about anything to me. He lifts me and slides a pillow under my hips.

I cry out when he surges inside me from behind. He's so big and so hard, and he goes so deep.

"You okay?" he asks, his voice right beside my ear. He covers me completely, and places his lips on my shoulder.

"More," I say. I push my bottom back against him, and he laughs and plunges deep. He lifts one knee out to the side, and adjusts his body so that he's going deeper than anyone has before. This time when I come, it's not a convulsive, body-shaking orgasm. It's a feeling of warmth that seeps from my center all the way to the tips of my fingers and my feet. I'm hot and satisfied, and he shoves all the way inside me one last time, and grunts in my ear.

"God, I love fucking you," he says as he pounds out his orgasm.

My nerves are raw and ragged, and I'm glad when he rolls off of me and lands by my side. He pulls the pillow from under me and I curl into his side, laying my head on his shoulder.

He kisses my forehead, tugs the covers up over us, and I fall asleep to the beat of his heart.

Sam

I get up the next morning and gently slide out from under Peck's sleeping body. She's wrapped around me so tight that her hand is tucked beneath me. I try not to wake her yet, because she has a bus to catch in an hour and I want her to get all the sleep she can get before leaving.

I get dressed quickly and go downstairs to get her some coffee at the hotel coffee shop. I don't even know if she likes coffee, but I'm guessing she'll need something to get her started.

There are tabloids next to the checkout counter and I freeze when I see that one is about the Zeroes. On the cover is a picture of Peck with her lips locked against a man. He has his arm wrapped around her waist and she's bent backward, he's kissing her so hard.

Heat travels up my body and floods my face. My hand shakes when I reach for the magazine. I buy it and the two coffees, and I go sit down at a table to read what it says.

Zeroes drummer fires opening act after lovers quarrel.

I flip the page to read where it's continued. There's more than one picture, and this one is just as compromising as the other. She was with someone else. Right before I married her. She was in someone else's arms. In someone else's bed. My gut clenches.

I thought we were a sure thing. I asked her to marry me, and she agreed. I thought that meant that we were engaged, and engaged usually means two people—not two people and occasionally someone else. And she definitely had someone else. He's wrapped all around her.

I fold the paper and put it in my back pocket, and then I pick up the coffees and go upstairs. When I get there, I can hear the shower running and she's singing softly to herself.

I pace from one side of the room to the other. I don't even know how to ask her about this.

I know that I feel like someone has laid me open. Like all my nerves are raw and exposed. Like I can't catch my breath.

The shower cuts off and she comes out wrapped in a towel. "There you are," she says with a smile.

I'm not smiling. "Were you going to tell me?" I demand.

She freezes, the smile gone. "Tell you what?"

"*Were you going to tell me?*" I ask again.

She stares at me. "No," she finally says. She blows out a breath. "I wasn't going to tell you."

I'm...floored. "Didn't you think I deserved to know?"

"I did, but I didn't want to hurt you." She sits down on the edge of the bed. "I'm sorry. If I had it to do over again, I'd do it differently."

"I can't believe you did this."

"Sam—"

"I thought I knew you."

"You do."

"I don't."

"You do!" she cries. She gets to her feet. "I'm sorry!" She shakes her head. "I can't say more than that. I can't undo it. And Logan..." Her voice trails off.

My heart stops beating. "Logan knew?"

Her brow creases with confusion. "What?"

"Never mind. I get it."

"I knew I should have told you!" she cries out. "I knew it. I should have gone with my gut. I should have told you. And I'll never make that mistake again." She walks forward and grabs my shirt in her fists. "I swear to you that I'll never do that again."

"I know you won't." *I won't give you the opportunity.*

Hot tears scald the backs of my eyes.

"Where are you going?" she asks as I walk toward the door.

I walk out without another word. And I can't go back. She just admitted that she betrayed me. She betrayed us, and to make it worse, Logan knew about it all the while.

I go out the front door and straight to the airport. I don't pass go. I don't collect two hundred dollars. And I leave my heart behind, shattered into a million pieces.

Peck

I knock on Logan's door, banging hard with the side of my fist. Suddenly, it flies open and Emily is standing on the other side. "What's wrong?" she asks.

I stumble into her room and look around. "Where is he?"

"Who?"

"Sam."

"Why would Sam be here?" Kit toddles over to me and holds up her arms. I pick her up, because I don't know what else to do. She pats the side of my face.

"He's not here?"

"Why would Sam be here?" she asks again, her voice stronger.

"He got mad and left." I start to pace. Kit doesn't seem to mind, and she lays her face on my shoulder. "Where would he go?"

"Why was he mad?" Emily is starting to worry. "Did something happen?"

"He didn't understand why I didn't tell him about Logan's surgery as soon as I found out. I knew I should have told him."

The door opens and I hold my breath when Logan walks in. He closes the door behind him and my heart drops. Sam is not with him.

Logan's looking at his phone. "I just got the weirdest text from Sam."

"What did it say?" I ask.

He reads: *Out of everyone, I never expected this from you.*

His thumbs are flying. I'd love to know what he's saying. Emily goes to his shoulder and reads aloud over it. *What are you talking about?*

You should have told me, Logan reads.

I already apologized for that, Emily reads.

You're my fucking brother.

What the fuck are you talking about?

Logan throws the phone on the bed and stomps into the bathroom. Emily snatches it up. "Uh-oh," she breathes. "I think there was a misunderstanding." She holds up the phone and shows me a tabloid cover on it that Sam has taken a picture of. It's a picture of me and the douche who kissed me after the show last night. I take the phone from her and stare hard at it.

"*That's* what he was talking about?" I look at her. "I thought he was asking me why I withheld the truth about Logan's implant! I admitted to it. Now I realize I admitted to—" I hold out the phone. "—this!" I throw the phone down on the bed and walk out.

I pull out my own phone in the hallway and dial Sam's number. He doesn't answer, so I leave a voicemail. "Sam, I think there was a misunderstanding. Please come back."

I text him.

Please call me. I didn't understand what you were talking about.

Nothing in response.

Please come back so we can talk about this.

I text him over and over.

I get nada.

Zip.

Zero.

Zilch.

Finally, it's time to get on the bus. Logan and Emily get on before me and set up their playpen and unload Kit's toys.

"Have you talked to him?" I ask Emily.

"No. He's not answering."

Logan is throwing luggage into the overhead bins a little too forcefully.

"What do I do?" I ask her.

"If he won't answer his phone, there's not much any of us can do." She glares at me. "You should have talked to him about it before he stormed out."

"I did!"

Emily doesn't even look at me, but Logan does.

"What do I do?" I ask him.

"Nothing. If he wanted to talk, he'd be talking." He goes into their little suite and closes the door.

A sob wells up in my throat. I climb into my bunk, which is about the size of a postage stamp, and pull the curtain shut. I sob into my pillow, hoping that none of them hear me. The curtain shuffles, and someone climbs in with me. There's barely enough space for one, much less two.

But Star has always climbed into bed with me. She has done it ever since we first became Zeroes, when she kept the monsters away. I'm afraid this is one monster she can't slay, though. She takes my hand in hers and doesn't say a word. She just lies there holding my hand.

***

A week later, Logan finally tells me where Sam is.

"He went back with the team. The doctor released him and he got his boot off, so he's training hard and traveling with the team."

"Oh."

"Are you okay?" Logan asks.

I shake my head. "Not really. Did you talk to him?"

"No, he's avoiding everyone. And since he's traveling, no one can go and kick him in the ass, although Paul is ready to burst into the stadium and drag him off the field just so he can do it."

"Will you tell me if you talk to him?"

He nods. "I will." He squeezes my shoulder.

I guess I just need to give him some time. I'll wait.

***

One week after that, Emilio and Marta show up at one of our tour stops. The door to the bus opens right before we're about to pull out, and Fin sees them first. She squeals and jumps up, wrapping her arms around Emilio. They all take turns getting hugs, and I've honestly never been so glad to see anyone in my life.

The minute Marta puts her arms around me, I burst into tears. "Let's talk," she says, rubbing my back.

We walk to the back of the bus, where there's a bench on one side. We sit down and she says, "Tell me what happened."

I explain it all, from top to bottom, from Logan's ears to the douchebag who kissed me, and she listens intently. "And now he's gone back to traveling with the team, so I couldn't find him to talk to him even if I tried." And I did try. I left message after message and sent numerous texts. I got nothing in response.

"Do you want to go to him?" she asks.

I nod. "I want to explain. I didn't cheat. I'm not that kind of person."

"I saw him."

"What?"

"Emilio was being a dad, and he tracked Sam to the stadium. Don't worry. He came out of it with nothing more than a black eye." She looks chagrined.

"Melio has a black eye?"

She shakes her head. "No, Sam does."

"*Melio hit him?*" I jump up and run to the front of the bus. "You hit him?"

Emilio gathers his hair in his hands and puts it in a ponytail. "Yep."

My sisters are all biting their lips to keep from smiling, I can tell. "Why would you do that?"

He shrugs. "Because I'm your father, and it's what fathers do. We protect our daughters."

I throw my hands up. "I can't believe you did that."

He gets up and points a finger in my face. "I did. And I'd do it again. Any man who makes one of my girls cry over something so fucking stupid deserves to get punched in the face. Hell, I should have punched him in the nuts. And I will if I ever get an opportunity." He sits back down, huffing.

I look up and see Logan leaning against the kitchenette counter. "He deserved it," he says. He holds out his phone. "He just texted me, by the way."

I follow Logan to the back of the bus. "What did he say?" I feel like a dog begging for a treat.

"Said he was sorry he misunderstood and he should have known better."

"Did he say anything about me?"

He shakes his head. "But he sent some tickets over. We're going to be in the same city as the team tomorrow. He wants us to come to the game." He shrugs. "It's our night off."

"Is there a ticket for me?" I ask.

Logan holds one up and it has my name written on it. My heart leaps.

But I shake my head anyway. "I'm not going. If he wanted to talk to me, he would have called or responded to one of my million texts."

Logan tucks the tickets in his pocket. "Whatever you want."

I go back to the bench and sit back down beside Marta. "I want to talk to you about your mother," she says.

"What about her?" I nibble on a fingernail. My mother is nowhere near the top of my thoughts.

"Honey, she overdosed again," she says quietly.

My heart aches for what could have been. "When is the funeral?"

She smiles. "Oh, she's not dead. Emilio checked her into rehab. Don't worry, he's paying for it."

"Oh."

"I went to talk to her."

"Why?" Why would she willingly do that? *Why?*

"Because I love you. That's why." I expect her to thump the back of my head any second, but she doesn't.

"What did she say?" My curiosity is growing.

"She's not remorseful. Not yet. Right now she's angry."

"Yeah, so am I."

"When you get home, I hope she's at a better place in her life and you can talk to her."

I shake my head.

"I *want* you to talk to her." She squeezes my hand.

"Okay."

I always do what Marta tells me to do. Because I know she loves me. I have never, ever doubted it. Not once.

"I had another visitor this week," she says. She stares hard at me.

I snort. "Who else is left?"

"Mrs. Derricks had a son. He came to see us." She makes a noise with her teeth. "He wanted to bring something for you." She reaches into her purse and pulls out a leather-clad book. "Apparently, Mrs. Derricks kept a journal about each of the kids she helped."

"Must have been a lot of books," I mumble.

Marta laughs. "This one is for you. He thought you might want it one day." She holds it out to me. I take it. Mrs. Derricks saved my life and I almost feel like reading her journal would be prying into her secrets. I'll save it.

"Read it," Marta says.

"I will."

"Read it now," she says. She motions toward my bunk. "Don't come out until you're done. Off with you, now."

Emilio bellows from the front of the bus. "Marta, come and play blackjack with us. And bring some cash! The girls won't let me play unless I have money!"

Marta rolls her eyes. She brushes her hand down the length of my hair.

"What about your car?" I ask.

She waves a breezy hand through the air. "Emilio paid some roadie to drive and follow the bus in it."

I laugh. Leave it to Melio to find a way around anything.

She points to my bunk again. "Go." She takes me by the shoulders and turns me around. Then she slaps my bottom. I climb into my bunk and roll onto my back. I flip the light on and open the journal. Then I start to read.

August 9

I met a young girl today. She's in second grade, and one of the teachers came to me with concerns. The girl barely speaks and the teacher was troubled about it. I met with Renee at lunchtime and asked her to come and see me in my office. She sat down in the chair across from my desk and swung her feet forward and back, but she didn't say a word. I wanted to engage her, but I didn't want to force her to talk, so I pretended to get a handful of change out of my purse and I dropped it all on the floor.

She immediately scurried onto all fours to help me pick it up. It broke the ice as we crawled around on our hands and knees. I asked her if she had any brothers or sisters, and she shook her head no. With more innocent questions, I finally managed to get her to say a few words.

The teacher was concerned not only about her lack of speech, but also about her home life. Just after talking with Renee for a moment, I realized that she had a debilitating stammer. She is troubled even by simple words, and works to get them out. More often than not, she gives up and just sits quietly.

But what bugs me most is that the teacher says she often comes to school with no lunch money. She rarely has breakfast and the teacher can hear her stomach growling. When she offers her food in secret, Renee gobbles it down like she's starving.

I keep boxes of crackers in my cabinet, so I took them out and Renee eyed them like she might a Thanksgiving dinner. I let her eat until she was full, and finally she started to talk. Her stammer is bad, but it's not so bad that I couldn't understand her. She is exceptionally bright, and she has a wonderful spirit. Her teachers say she is quiet in class, but helpful and polite. But I know that she is hurting. Don't ask me how I know, but I do. I can see it in her eyes. In her soul. And I am going to help her if it's the last thing I ever do.

I wipe a tear from my lashes.

September 7 (one year later)

I worried about Renee all summer. Did she have enough to eat? Did she have someone to read books to her? Did she have clean clothes? Was she alone?

When I saw her today, I was relieved. She came into my office, went to the cabinet, and sat down across from me with a box of crackers. She ate while we talked. She assured me that things are fine at home, but I know she's lying. I know something is wrong.

October 10
I made a home visit to Renee's house today. I know I'm not supposed to unless I'm on official school business, but I couldn't help it. I wanted to see where she lives. I knocked on the door and waited, and Renee herself came and let me in. She smiled and looked relieved when she saw me, so I held up the fast food bag of hamburgers I'd brought with me. She took it and went to the table, where she set two places—one for me and one for her.
"That's all for you," I told her.
"But I w-want to share. You'll stay l-longer if you have a full t-tummy."
She was worried that I would leave.
"Where's your mom?" I asked.
"She's at w-work. She'll be home l-later."
"Are you alone?"
She smiled. "Not right n-now. You're here."
I left soon after that, but I sat outside until I saw her mother come home around midnight. She stumbled to the door, let herself in, and then I could see Renee put her to bed a few minutes later. Finally, Renee pulled the curtains, and I couldn't see anything else.
I went home with a heavy heart.

December 12
I feel really bad about doing it, but I reported Renee's living situation to Social Services today. She's alone almost all of the time. She doesn't have a babysitter, and she has to come to my office every day just so she can have lunch. I have started bringing twice the food for lunch just so I can feed her.

I never knew she did that. She always told me she just wasn't hungry.

December 23

Renee came to my office today. She was carrying a tiny package wrapped in tissue paper. "M-m-merry C-c-christmas," she finally got out. I took it and exclaimed over the beautiful wrapping, and she blushed, but she was pleased too, I could tell.

I opened it up to find a small clay dish. I know all the kids made them in art class as presents for their parents, but this one was special. I flipped it over and saw her name etched in pencil on the bottom.

"I can't take this," I told her. "You should give it to someone you love." I tried to hand it back to her, although I wanted to keep it more than anything.

"I d-did," she said quietly. Then she left my office. I probably won't see her again until the new year.

I read and read and read, wiping tears from my eyes as I turn the pages. I stop when I get to four years later.

March 4

Social Services had to take action today. They have done numerous home visits over the past four years, but Renee keeps falling through the cracks. Her mother refuses to put her in speech therapy, and I am still feeding her every day (although, truly, I don't want to stop that, ever). That little girl has more compassion in her little finger than most people have in their whole body. I envy her. I envy the fact that she can take so little and turn it into so much.

But Social Services couldn't ignore it four days ago when Renee had an attack of appendicitis. I had to take her to the hospital myself and no one could find her mother. For four days, they searched. Renee didn't seem to mind. She is apparently used to it.

She's currently in a group home. It hurts my heart to know that she's there, but she needs to be somewhere that someone can care for her. I stop by every few days just to be sure she's okay, and she's still smiling.

The girls who share her room are some characters. The five of them have formed a bond. I'm glad she has them in her life. And I hope a family comes forward for her soon, because if anyone deserves a happy life, it's this little girl.

(four months later)

I went to the courthouse today to watch the Vasquez family finalize the proceedings for adoption. They didn't adopt just Renee. They adopted all five of the girls. They asked her if she wanted to take their last name, and she said she wanted a new first and last name, not just a last name. So they talked it out, and all five girls get brand new starts. I know with all my heart that Renee—no, she's not Renee anymore—I know that Peck will be loved beyond boundaries. She will be cherished. She will be fed. She will be protected.

She's learning to play the drums, and I'm so proud of her. She goes after what she wants. I wish everyone had her strength and the ability to persevere.

My only wish for her is that she holds on to that fighting spirit, for it will take her far.

There are a few more entries, like the one about our first concert. She was on the front row at that one, screaming louder than anyone in the auditorium.

(the last entry)

Peck is all grown up. She's strong, faithful, and most of all, she is loved. My job is done. I will go home tonight and hug my own son a little harder. And I will pray that if he ever finds himself alone, that someone will step up to help him.

Peck, when she finally settles down and marries, will need someone as strong-willed as she is, but someone who has a gentle side. She needs someone who will cherish the words that still stick on her tongue, and someone who will be okay with it if she just sits quietly. He will have to be a special man, but I doubt any of it will come easily. She will have to fight for the right one. I just hope she's capable. I hope she doesn't let fear or doubt overwhelm her. I hope she goes for it. Because I know she can.

I crawl out of my cubby and wipe my face. Everyone is at the table playing poker. Marta looks at me with her eyes shining. "All done?" she asks.

I nod and sniff back a tear. I look at Logan. "Can I have that ticket?"

He pulls it out of his back pocket and grins at me. "I'll see you there?" he asks.

Oh, yes, he will most definitely see me there. The whole world is going to see me.

Sam

It feels funny playing again. I stretch my leg and try not to hop on it. It's not even tender, but my trainer says I have a tendency to lay off it, and I'm sure he's right.

We run onto the field and I can't keep from looking into the stands. I sent her a ticket via Logan, but I really don't expect her to use it. Hell, I wouldn't use it if I was her. I would tell me to go fuck myself after the way I acted. I deserve it. But my heart stalls a little when I see her empty seat. Logan and Emily are here, and all of her sisters used their tickets. I wave at them from the sidelines and point to her empty seat. Star shrugs her shoulders and grimaces. Emilio holds up his fist like he wants to hit me again. I still have a black eye from the last time.

I head to gather with my team on the sidelines.

It's cold and my breath comes out in tiny little puffs of steam. Wherever Peck is, I hope she has a coat. The whistle blows and the clock starts, and I no longer have time to think about her. I think about football. I get to hit people. And knock people down. I get to run and play this sport I love, professionally. I am lucky and I know it.

But I still wish she was here.

Peck

The guy looks like I'm inconveniencing him, but I don't care. I had to grease some serious palms to get this to work.

"There's a two-minute warning time out right before the end of the half. The cameras will go to a commercial, but I can get you on the Jumbotron. You'll have about forty-five seconds. That's all. Nothing more. After that, the play will resume. So he won't see anything you have to say after that."

"I got it."

My palms are sweaty, and even though it's really cold out tonight, I'm hot all over. I'm nervous. So nervous. What if he doesn't care? What if he doesn't want me to make a grand gesture? What if…

I shake my head. Mrs. Derricks believed I could do this. She believed I could be fearless, and she was never wrong. She was the first person who ever believed in me, and I'm not about to let her down. And I'm not going to let Sam go without a fight.

I make my way out to my seat, and I see that my sisters have already done their job because all the people sitting around are holding signs down by their feet, and they cheer when I show up. I duck my head and grin. I'm so embarrassed. A few people pat me on the shoulder as I walk into the center of them all.

"I guess they're all ready, huh?" I ask Star.

"Primed and ready," she says. She grins. "I am so jealous."

I snort. "Because I'm about to make a spectacle of myself?"

Her face softens. "No, because you're in love."

I blink back tears.

I watch the clock, and two minutes before the two-minute warning that will signal the commercial break time out before the end of the half, everyone in our section stands up and holds their signs up above their heads. From a distance, it looks like a solid sign. The crowd in our section starts to chant, "Fifty-one! Look over here!" *Stomp!* *Stomp!* "Fifty-one! Look over here!" *Stomp! Stomp!*

They chant it until it spreads to other sections and people start to point and pick up the sound. You can hear it roar around the stadium. The Jumbotron picks us up, and I see my section on the big screen. The signs, when all put together, read: *51, look here!*

A smaller screen near us pans to Sam. He's pacing back and forth down the sideline, and he's not even looking in our direction. But then one of his teammates smacks him on the shoulder and he looks toward me. He stops.

He unstraps his helmet, pulls it from his head and stares up at me.

Star motions for everyone in our section to be quiet, and they all lower their signs. Emily swipes a tear from her cheek and says, "Go for it." Logan wraps an arm around her and Kit and holds them tight. Logan is grinning like a fool, though.

The camera guy is right in front of me. "Forty-five seconds," he reminds me. I see my image on the big screen and one of the guys on the field points to it, so Sam looks in that direction.

I hold up my signs. I have them grouped in order, one after the other. I show the first one.

I love you, 51!

I flip to the next.

I don't want to be just a Zero anymore.

Flip.

I want to be a Zero-plus-one.

Flip.

Or a Zero-plus-two.

Flip.

Maybe even a Zero-plus-three.

Flip.

I want to make little cupcakes with you.

Flip.

Only you.

Flip.

Forever.

Flip.

Check yes or no.

I take this last card and walk out of my section. I have hands of people I don't even know reaching out to steady me, and they're all saying encouraging things. The camera guy runs along behind me, cursing as he chases me down the stairs.

I run with my last card all the way down to the bottom bleacher and I lean over the side, holding it down against the concrete block wall. I pull a marker from my pocket and hold it out, too.

Then I wait. It's the longest forty-five seconds of my life.

Sam stands completely still.

He scratches his head.

His teammates say things to him and he still stands there.

The clock is ticking. Maybe he doesn't want what I want after all.

Then he starts to run toward me. He jogs in my direction, and my heart is in my throat. I have tears running down my face, and I don't care.

When he gets to the wall, he stares up at me. There's no way he can come up this high, so I drop the board with the check boxes and the pen on the ground in front of him. He grins up at me and lays the board on the grass. He takes the pen and starts to check a box. Then he stops and looks up. Then he moves like he's finally going to do it. Then he stops and looks up. I'm going to kick his ass if he keeps messing with me. Then he checks the *yes* box and holds the board up for the whole stadium to see.

The buzzer goes off and he has to run with his teammates back onto the field to play the last two minutes of the half. When that's over, just before he goes into the tunnel, he turns back and flashes me the *I love you* sign, along with a big smile. My heart settles.

I can't wipe the grin from my face as I go back to my seat and sit down. Marta lays a hand on my back. "I knew you could do it," she says.

"I'm glad you did, because I wasn't sure."

For the rest of the game, I accept congratulations from complete strangers. It's chaotic and wonderful and at the center of it all, there is a sense of peace. Of wellbeing. A feeling like I am where I should be.

Sam

I step out of the locker room and run into one of my teammates. My hair is damp from my shower and I don't care. I just want to see her. I can't imagine how tough that was for her to make a public declaration like that. She has more balls than I gave her credit for.

"Dude," my teammate says. "Watch where you're going." But he's grinning. "You still got your head in the clouds."

I grin. "Yeah."

Then I turn the corner and I see her standing there. She's leaning against the wall, her hip hitched against the concrete. Her coat is slung over her crossed arms, and she smiles shyly at me when she sees me. I hold up the *check-yes-or-no* sign, because I saved it. I'm going to keep it forever. Her cheeks go rosy. She ducks her head like she's suddenly shy.

I'm grinning like a damn fool, and I don't care.

I jog over to her and stop just before I can touch her.

"Hi," she says.

"What's up?" I reply, but I can't smother my grin.

"I don't know." She rolls a rock with the toe of her shoe.

"I'm glad you're here," I tell her. I push a lock of hair behind her ear.

"Are you?" Her voice is so quiet that I can barely hear her.

I nod.

Then I grab her. I can't help it. I grab her and pull her against me. I need to feel her, to touch her, to smell her. I kiss her, because I really need to taste her. I hear the tiny little noises she makes when she's excited, and she growls against my lips.

The coach barks out, "Knock it off, Reed!"

I lift my head, but I imagine I have stars flying around my head like Sylvester the cat after he gets hit with a rolling pin.

"But she's Mrs. Reed, coach!" I call back.

"Congratulations," he says drolly. But he's smiling too. "Now get a room."

My phone dings in my pocket. I pull it out and laugh. It's a text from Paul.

I show her the phone and she blushes. *Use a condom*, it says.

"Hope you have a whole box," she whispers.

My eyebrows are probably near my hairline at that remark. I grab her hand and take her to the exit, where we catch a cab back to the hotel. "When do you leave?" I ask.

"In the morning," she says sadly.

"Me too." I pull her legs across my lap because I just can't stop touching her.

"How's your leg?" she asks.

I nod. "Better."

I nuzzle my nose into her neck and she giggles. She touches my eye, which is still a little purple from her father's fist. "Sorry about that," she says.

I shake my head. "Don't be. When we have a kid, I'm going to be the same way."

"So…" she says slowly.

"So…you want to make cupcakes with me, huh?" I grin.

"Yep. I want to adopt one, too."

I nod and pull her closer. "Okay."

We get to the hotel room finally. She doesn't wait. She starts stripping off her clothes. She's not bashful at all. Not a bit. When she's naked, she struts over to me. "So…you want to start on those cupcakes tonight?"

I pick her up and toss her onto the bed. "Hell yeah."

She's so beautiful, all spread out on my bed. Her breasts are heavy and they hang to the side a little. She spreads her thighs while I watch and dips her finger into her pussy, then brings it up and swirls it around her clit.

I fall onto the bed between her thighs and replace her hand with my lips. She threads her fingers into my hair, and the little noises she's making nearly undo me. I arch my hips against the bed, trying to soothe my aching dick. I haven't so much as even thought about coming since the last time I saw her, and my balls are aching to sink inside her. And immediately disgrace myself.

I part her folds with my fingers and suck her clit into my mouth, lapping at it with insistence while I suckle her tender flesh. She cries out, and I slide two fingers inside her. Almost immediately, she squeezes around my fingers and comes. Her hands in my hair hold me against her pussy, and I make my lips more tender as she comes down from her orgasm.

"Forgive me in advance," I tell her, as I hold her legs wide and push my way inside her. I bring her feet together on my left shoulder, and she's so tight like this that I can barely get inside her. "But I'm going to come really quick."

My balls tickle and I can already feel the pull of my orgasm, and I try to hold off, but then she takes my finger into her mouth and sucks on it while I fuck her, and I need to come.

"Can I come inside you?" I ask.

She pants. But she nods. And I do.

I feel like she has split me open and laid me bare. Like she's seeing every part of me as I pour myself into her.

I let her legs drop, then I fall to her side, and she rolls toward me.

I flip over to face her and draw a circle on her bicep. "I'm really sorry," I tell her, but she covers my mouth with her hand.

"It's okay."

"It's not." It's really not.

"It's okay."

"I misunderstood and I should have given you time to explain." She's still and she listens as I explain my thoughts that day. I thought she cheated. And I know she didn't. If anybody knows how the tabloids can skew a story, it's me. "I'm sorry," I say again when I'm done.

"I love you," she says. She kisses me.

"I love you too." I kiss her back. "Can you stay tonight?"

She nods. "You can't get rid of me that easily."

"I don't want to ever get rid of you." I brush her hair back. I lean close and sniff her. I've missed everything about her. "You smell so good."

I roll her beneath me and take her nipple into my mouth. When she starts to squirm under me, I lift my head. "If you thought you were going to get any sleep tonight, you were wrong."

She laughs. "I like being wrong," she says as she reaches down between my legs.

Sam

He's only supposed to have one person with him, because of the amount of distraction lots of people can provide, but the audiologist lets us all go in the room with him. They even bring in more chairs for us all. He told us he didn't need for us *all* to be there.

"Where you go, we go," Paul says.

Emily is the only woman here. All the others opted to stay home, because the room just wasn't big enough for all of us. So it's me, Pete, Paul, and Matt, along with Emily and Kit. Kit's playing with some toys that Emily dropped in the corner of the room.

Logan's knees are jumping with nervousness, and I'm not sure he could sit still if he tried.

I remember when Logan lost his hearing. Our mom was devastated and worried and hopeful all at once. But she rushed right out and bought videos to teach us all sign language. We learned to sign and we learned how to live with a deaf person, how to adjust to his new life. But for us, Logan was just Logan, and we did what it took to communicate with him, and we didn't see it as more difficult than that.

This cochlear implant will certainly be a change, that's for sure.

The audiologist attaches the receiver using a magnet they implanted in Logan's head. "So you can't walk through metal detectors anymore, huh?" Pete asks.

Logan rolls his eyes at him and he puts on the behind the ear microphones. They look a lot like his hearing aids do.

Logan's knee is still bobbing up and down, and Emily covers it with her hand. She's sitting right beside him. He stops moving and looks at her. She stares back, and so much love passes between them that it makes me want to go home to Peck. Right this very second.

"You okay?" Paul asks Logan. He signs while he talks.

"Scared," Logan says back.

"I'm going to play a series of clicks for you, and I want you to tell me when you hear them, okay?" The audiologist waits for him to nod.

The room goes completely silent, and even Paul is holding his breath.

Logan's head jerks when he hears the clicks. "I hear it," he says. "Good," the audiologist says. "Is it loud?"

"No. Very quiet." He grins. "My voice is loud, though. Really loud." He looks at Emily. "Is my voice always this loud, Em?" He blushes. "I can hear my voice."

"It's going to sound really loud to you until you get used to it." The audiologist adjusts some knobs. "I'm going to play some beeps. Tell me when you hear them."

Logan's leg starts to jump again, and Emily covers it with her hand. He grabs her fingers and squeezes tight, smiling at her. His head jerks again and he laughs. "I hear it." He looks at everyone else. "Do you hear it, too?"

Paul nods. "We hear it."

"Holy cow!" Logan yells. "Is that your voice?" He stares at Paul.

I watch Paul as he blinks. His eyes form shallow little puddles and he looks away. "Yeah, that's my voice." He clears his throat. I look over at Pete and try to catch his eye so I can make fun of Paul tearing up, but he's swiping a hand across his cheek.

Logan grins. "I can hear you talking."

"It's going to take some time to get used to the sounds," the audiologist tells me. "You'll learn what sounds go with what items in the coming months. There might be sounds you don't recognize at all."

He points to Paul. "I heard his voice." Then Logan's eyes well up. "Sometimes I dream of your voice, Paul," he says. "It doesn't sound like that at all right now, but I still know it's you."

Paul gets up and goes to look out the window, facing the other way.

Matt pulls a tissue from a box on the desk and blots his face, and then he passes the box around. He has been videoing the whole thing so Logan will have it later.

Logan turns to Emily. She's actually holding it together a lot better than the men in the room. I blow my nose into a tissue as he tells her, "Talk to me, Em. Say something."

She reaches out and cups the side of his face. "Oh, Logan," she says. And a tear finally falls over her lashes and down her cheek. "I love you so much."

"I love you too," he says back.

And finally, he drops his head into his hands and cries.

Paul pushes the tissue box into his hands and kneels down in front of him. "You okay?" he asks gently.

"Yeah." Logan breathes out a heavy sigh. "I didn't expect to be this emotional."

"Neither did we," Pete adds. He coughs to clear his thick throat.

Kit gets up and walks over to Logan, and she pats his arm. He looks down at her. "Hi," he says.

So far, she's only said *ma ma ma ma ma ma* and some other simple sounds. But she's never said anything else. She holds out her toy and he takes it from her. He picks her up and puts her on his knee. "Da da da da da da," she says.

Logan's eyes roam quickly from one of us to another. "Did you hear that?"

"Did *you* hear that?" the audiologist asks.

"She said da da da da da." He's almost shivering with emotion. I can feel it all the way in my seat.

"Yes, she did."

Kit shakes her toy and Logan jumps. He takes it from her and shakes it again. "That was this?" He gives it back to her. "It's loud."

"Now you see why I don't want to buy her things with batteries," Emily tosses out.

"I see it. And I hear it." Logan grins.

The audiologist goes through some things with Logan, and we all pay attention, because we want to know all we can. But what we leave with is Logan, *and he's hearing.* He may not hear the same way we do, but he can hear sounds.

"The birds are singing?" he asks as he we walk outside.

A car horn blares from the street and he jumps about a foot in the air. "What was that?"

"Car." Matt pats his shoulder. "Speaking of which, we need to get a cab."

Logan looks at Emily. "You feel like walking back?"

Kit is in her stroller and she's all warm in her winter coat. "Sure." She grins. "We can walk all you want."

Logan steps on a metal drain on the cement, and it makes a noise. He stops and rocks his foot so that it will do it again. "That's cool," he says.

Paul says, "Thanks for letting us come with you."

"Where I go, you go. Where you go, I go." Logan grabs Paul and hugs him.

"Always," Paul says close to his ear.

Logan's eyes close for a second. Then he says, "Always."

Oh fuck, now they're going to make me cry.

"You guys should grab a cab," Logan says.

Paul shakes his head. "We'll walk with you."

And the five of us, and Emily and Kit, start walking. Logan stops to figure out noises as we go, and it's like watching him experience it all for the first time. I wouldn't have missed it for the world.

Epilogue
Peck

Sam puts the finishing touches on a plate and slides it toward a waiter, who takes it and dashes out of the kitchen to go serve it.

"There's a line around the building. Again," Paul says as he walks into the kitchen. He has a towel slung over his arm and a notepad in his hand. "I need one special and one Chicken Parmigiana." He passes the order to Sam and Sam growls.

"I wish they would try some of the new items on the menu."

Paul shrugs. "They know what they like."

Sam's restaurant opened just over a month ago, and it has been busy every day, all day. He hired a manager to run it, but he spends a lot of time here. He wouldn't have it any other way.

"How are you feeling?" Paul asks me. He lays a hand on my belly and the baby does a roll. Paul laughs. "I'm surprised you haven't popped yet."

I was due three days ago. Sam refused to leave me alone tonight, just in case.

Sam's contract was up for renewal at the end of the season, and he decided not to renew. He gave up the chance of big bucks playing a game he loves in order to pursue his dream of his own restaurant. We didn't like being apart when I'm on tour, and we were just spending too much time without one another. At least now he can let his manager run Reeds' and he can travel with me.

Sam looks up and sees Paul's hand on my belly. "Everything okay?" he asks. His brow furrows.

I wave a hand in the air. "I'm fine. Keep doing what you're doing."

On busy nights, all the Reed boys pitch in to help serve. They like doing it, and they get to see people in the community and bullshit with everyone. They love it, and Sam is grateful they're here.

Logan walks into the room and Sam yells his name. He looks over and says, "What?"

I can't get used to the fact that Logan can hear. It's still strange to call his name and have him look at us.

"Take my wife and find her a seat somewhere, will you?" He doesn't look up from the plate he's preparing.

"Your wife is fine," I say.

Logan grabs a chair and hits me in the backs of the legs with it, so I sit. He grins and kisses my forehead.

Josh rolls into the kitchen and stops. "Um, Sam…"

Sam looks up.

"We have a little problem out here."

"What is it?"

"Um…one of Peck's sisters is dancing on the piano."

I rush out into the dining area and find, of all people, Star standing on top of the piano. She's dancing to music only she can hear. She's not bad, actually. Now she just needs a pole.

Three of my sisters are trying to help her get down, but she won't.

"What's wrong with her?" I ask as I walk up to my sisters.

Fin looks at me and says, "We don't know. She showed up like this."

"Where's Wren?" I ask.

Fin shrugs. "No one has been able to find her."

Crap. I'm actually a lot more worried about Star than I am about Wren. One thing you have to understand about Star is that she always looks perfect on the outside. We know she's not perfect on the inside. None of us are, but on the outside, she always keeps up the façade. Always. Something terrible must have happened.

Sam walks up beside me. "What the fuck…?"

"Get her down, Sam," I beg him, tugging on his sleeve.

He motions her forward. "Hey Star," he says gently. "I have something I need to show you."

"If it's your dick," she replies, "the answer is no, thank you."

Her speech is slurred and she can barely stand up.

Suddenly, Sam grabs her leg and she almost falls, but he adjusts her body so that she falls across his shoulder.

He hitches her ass higher and walks to the door. Josh grabs her purse and her coat from her table, and he rolls outside with us.

Suddenly, a pain shoots across my middle and warm water gushes at my feet. "Um, Sam…"

He puts Star in a cab and pays the driver. "Do you want to go with her?" he asks.

Well, that was my plan until right this minute. I look down at my feet. "I don't think I can."

"Oh, shit. It's time?" he cries.

"Go get one of my sisters to go with her." I motion him forward. "And hurry."

Sam disappears inside.

We need to call Emilio, too, so he can find Wren.

Star gets out of the cab and the driver must see the futility of this mission, because he takes off.

"Well, shit," Josh says.

Josh just got out of jail. He certainly doesn't need any trouble, not even when it's one of my sisters.

"I got her," I say. I grab her elbow, but a pain suddenly hits me.

"Oh, fuck!" Star cries. "You're having a fucking baby!" She cups her hands around her mouth. "I'm going to be the best aunt ever!" she yells.

She starts to jump up and down, and her ankle gives out. She really shouldn't be on those stilts when she's drunk. She hops a little. She's going to feel that ankle tomorrow. "I think I just hurt myself," she says, and her eyes well up with tears. "I think I need to sit down." Then she plops her ass right down in Josh's lap.

"You're a lump, aren't you?" he says to her as he adjusts her body for comfort.

"Are you calling me fat?" She looks at him over her shoulder.

He grins and shakes his head. "Only in the best possible way."

Sam runs out of the restaurant and he is dangling keys in his hand. "You ready?" he asks. He looks at Star, who is in Josh's lap. "What's up with that?" he asks. "Get her in the car," he says to Paul.

"You guys should go ahead," Josh says. "I'll get some coffee into Star."

"We should take her with us," I say, but Sam cuts me off.

"Josh will sober her up and bring her to the hospital later, right, Josh?"

"Yep." Josh looks warily down her top, which has somehow lost a button. He fixes her up and buttons her up to her throat.

Star wiggles her bottom in his lap. "Are you getting a boner?" she asks with a giggle.

He grunts, picks her ass up and slides her over. "Be still," he warns.

"You are, aren't you? I was worried all your parts didn't work, but apparently…" She waggles her brows at him.

Another pain slices through my middle. "We should go. Now."

"Oh!" Sam cries.

"Josh, are you sure you can take care of Star?"

He looks up at me and smiles. "You can trust me. I'll take care of her."

I believe him. And so does Sam.

Paul leans into the car after we're inside. "We'll stay here and close up, and meet you there."

Sam nods. He lays a hand on my belly. "You ready for this, cupcake?" he asks as Paul slams the door.

I cover his hand with mine and the baby kicks. My whole belly rocks. "Yeah. I'm ready."

***

They settle us into a room, and Emilio and Marta show up. Emilio looks scared and Marta is glowing. She adjusts my covers. "Not much longer now."

"Did you find Wren?" I ask.

Marta nods but she doesn't look me in the eye. "She's fine."

Marta was right. Only a few short hours later and they tell me to *push*.

Sam holds my hand as pain streaks through my body. "This had better be the last one," I gasp.

And suddenly, there's a head.

Sam is the only visitor in the delivery room, and he looks down and his face goes ashen.

"What's wrong?" I ask.

"That's disgusting and beautiful all at the same time." His eyes are shining with tears. "We have a son, Peck. A son!"

"Dad, do you want to cut the cord?" the doctor asks.

Sam takes the scissors and cuts the cord, and they get me all cleaned up while they check the baby over.

"He's doing great," a nurse tells me as she puts him in my arms.

Suddenly, the room floods with Reeds and Zeroes. There's barely any air left for me to breathe, there are so many of them. But this is my life. It's the life I chose, and I wouldn't have it any other way.

Melio takes the baby and holds him. "I won't know what to do with a boy," he says. He wipes a tear from his eye.

"You'll figure it out," Marta says, patting him on the back. "We're grandparents." She lets out a shaky breath and comes to kiss my forehead. "I'm so proud," she whispers.

Soon, the room clears out, after everyone has passed the baby around the room at least once. Only my sisters are left.

"Where are Star and Wren?" I ask Fin.

"Star is in the waiting room."

"Why didn't she come in?"

Fin avoids my eyes. "She's waiting."

"What's wrong?"

She leans down and whispers in my ear. "Something happened with their brother, but they won't tell us what." She brushes my baby's hair from his forehead. "This has got to be the most beautiful baby I've ever seen," she says.

"Is Josh still with Star?" I ask. And where the heck is Wren?

She nods. "But I think he's staying under duress. No one else can do anything with Star." She gives me a reassuring look and nods. "Don't worry. They're fine. You concentrate on this beautiful little thing." She kisses Samuel Emilio on the head.

Sam scoots into the bed with me and puts his arm around me. "You're not a Zero anymore," he whispers. "You're a Zero-plus-two."

I kiss him, because emotion is clogging my throat so much that I can't speak.

I like being a Zero, because as a Zero, I knew I would never be alone. But now I have more than I ever dreamed possible. I have Sam. I have it all.

Once everyone has gone home, the door opens and Star comes in. She doesn't say a word. She just climbs into bed with me and I take her hand. She lies on one side and Sam is on the other with the baby in his arms. He doesn't get up. He looks at me and arches a brow, asking if I want him to leave. I don't. I never want him to leave.

Star lies there quietly, not saying a word, and I can feel the tension seeping out of her body. Finally, she goes to sleep, and I just lie there and hold her hand. I have no idea what happened today, but it had to be big.

The door opens and Wren's colorful head pops into the room. "Am I too late?" she asks. Her eyes roam from Star to me and back. "I was out looking for her," she says. "Glad I finally found her. Only Star would end up at the place where I should have been all along." She snorts, but it's a humorless sound.

"Everything okay?" I ask.

She shakes her head. "Not really. But it will be."

"It always is," I remind her.

She wipes a thumb beneath her nose. "Why does it have to take so damn long to get there sometimes, though?" she asks.

I look into Sam's blue eyes. "It's worth all the trouble."

He smiles at me and puts our baby into my arms.
Totally worth it.

AUTHOR'S NOTE

Dear readers,

When I started writing the Reed Brothers series, I tried to pitch it to a few major publishers, and the response I got was, "Are you going to fix his hearing by the end of the book?" My answer was a definite *no*. That's one of the many reasons I ended up going indie with this book. I felt very strongly that there was nothing wrong with Logan and he didn't need to be "fixed." He just needed the right girl, just like every other man-whore needs, right? That's what he was to me. He was a man who slept with a lot of women and he needed to find the right one that might make him want to settle down. His deafness was no more important to me than his eye color or his hair color. Just like Emily's dyslexia didn't define her. It was a characteristic, but not a definition.

I felt this way all the way up to when I was writing *Beautiful Bride*. Logan made a comment in BB that made me think. His character had changed, and he had different goals from the goals he had when I first created him.

He mentioned to Emily that he wanted to be able to hear his daughter laugh. That he wanted to share in her first words. His goals and dreams had changed. He wanted to be different.

Different. Not better. In no way am I implying that he needed to be *fixed*. He made the courageous decision to get a cochlear implant, which is often frowned upon in deaf culture.

For my character, this was the right choice. It's not the right choice for everyone, and I wouldn't even suggest it to most of the deaf people I know.

I felt like I clearly needed to explain my position on deafness and implants, so that readers understand how Logan ended up going in that direction. He didn't get it because I as the author felt like there was anything wrong with him.

Now that my explanation is out of the way, I want to answer a few reader questions:

Will Seth get a book?
Yes! But he needs to get a little older first.

How many more books are in this series?
I have Lark, Fin, Star, Wren, and Seth left. Not to mention Edward and Gonzo. I don't know how their lives will turn out, but I think they deserve a happily-ever-after too, don't you? Oh, and there's still Jack and Malone from *Only One*.

Thank you all for hanging in there with me! I've had so much fun writing this series, and I love interacting with you all on Facebook and Twitter. You can find me here:
Facebook
Twitter
And if you'd like to sign up for the mailing list, you can find it here.

Best regards,
Tammy Falkner

The Reed Brothers Series

Made in the USA
Lexington, KY
23 January 2015